MERON

The Survivor Amid The Pandemic

“To Mum.

As you always carry the thought of me, now I bear your memory.”

CHAPTER ONE

She was breathless and unconscious, lying flat on a bed, admitted to emergency room at St. Michael's University Hospital. Her cute and long hair stirred in motion with the vibratory movement of her chest. Ten minutes lapsed. The fast and deeper chest compressions synchronized with positive pressure ventilation didn't seem to be working. The likelihood that she was not going to make it fluctuated between 40% and 88%, depending on the underlying cause of her problem, which had to be yet determined.

Doctor Samuel saw it the other way round. His prediction about the chance of survival for his female patient was 60%. From his experience as a physician for 8 years, he knew that high-quality cardiopulmonary resuscitation (CPR) with emphasis on appropriate chest compression rate, depth, and recoil does increase the likelihood of successful return of spontaneous circulation and survival, following in-Hospital cardiac arrest.

He had high index of suspicion that the cause of cardiac arrest in his patient was beatable. He couldn't however convince the other physicians who labeled her COVID-X case. They genuinely believed that doing cardiopulmonary resuscitation to that patient would be meaningless.

They saw the 88% of likelihood that the patient wasn't going to survive up on receiving CPR. Almost non-salvageable patient and high risk of COVID-19 infection exposure. They had a big fear that Samuel couldn't quell, with all the strength of his argument and the depth of knowledge he had. In that moment of life or death for his patient, Samuel's focus was on the effect, not the cause. The patient's beauty shinned in the absence of oxygen. He didn't want that beauty to rust in grave.

Most of all, he didn't want to lose her as his patient, regardless whether she would remain beautiful or not. Resuscitate. Revive. Recover. Those were the only available words in his brain, at that critical moment of saving life.

Built on an acre of land at Bole district in Addis Ababa and with a capacity of 1000 beds –out of which were 10 intensive care unit beds, St. Michael's University Hospital was nominated as the leading medical college in Ethiopia a year ago. In the same year, Doctor Samuel completed his post- graduate obstetrics and gynaecology training.

The University was founded twenty-five years back. It had counted only six years since it launched post - graduate residency and two years since it began running fellowship training programs. One of the youngest colleges in Ethiopia and yet the best. St. Michael's University Hospital had a five years vision to ascend to the level of becoming the best medical school in East Africa.

Splendid view of Hospital infrastructure was one blessing that belonged to St. Michael's University Hospital. Medical training and health service of top-quality was the other, which made it qualify to be at the top of teaching Hospitals rankings in Ethiopia.

Whole block ground plus three main building, with a penthouse roofed over with a Cathedral ceiling, housed majority of the health service units of the Hospital. Sequentially, from third floor to the bottom, the building accommodated surgery department followed by internal medicine then paediatrics, and the department of obstetrics and gynaecology at the ground floor.

Being of the same height to the main building, its floors enclosed in suspended ceilings, the other two small apartment- like buildings stood on the northern and southern sides of the main building. Those buildings accommodated undergraduate and post-graduate teaching halls, registrar office, laboratory, radiology unit, and meeting halls.

Almost a football field sized front yard extended from the entrance gate of the Hospital up to the corridor of the ground floor of the main building. Decorated with flowers in different colors and palm trees and filled with a pleasant smell, from edge to edge, the garden area at the front yard was said to be a soul treatment for patients.

From above, a gray narrow street made up of concrete could be seen cutting its way through the garden area to the emergency department of the Hospital, with a branch connected to a large parking lot on the right side.

The whole compound of the University Hospital glittered a hilarious aesthetic beauty which filtered air pollution, as much as it saved the wards of the hospital from the noise of the mega city. The highways that run nearby was far away to deliver traffic roar to the inside of the Hospital.

CHAPTER TWO

To: *Post graduate Fellowship Program Director*

Re: *Motivation letter*

Dear program director,

My genuine interest to join the family planning fellowship training arose from a story about death of a beautiful woman from complications of unsafe abortion. And I was in the middle of the story.

The day was in December 2012. A 25 years old pregnant lady presented to gynaecology OPD at a district Hospital at gestational age of 21 weeks. She came in seeking safe abortion service. I was the physician (general practitioner) in charge of the OPD. She stated that the pregnancy was unwanted and unplanned. She had a boyfriend, whom with she continued to have an affair after she was engaged to another man in an arranged marriage, scheduled with a pressure from her parents.

Very unfortunate for her because she became pregnant before the wedding day, amid the confusion. What is more, I declined her of her right to have a safe abortion care. She looked depressed. She reported that she had suicidal attempt, twice. I made a terrible mistake then. I couldn't make a sound clinical judgment about where her problem could dangerously take her to. I failed at both ends. I declined her of her reproductive health right, which was safe abortion care. I was also reluctant to link her to another physician who could provide her desired health service.

Dreadfully, the woman returned a week later with a serious complication of unsafe abortion. She had septic abortion and severe sepsis was taking her life away as I watched it. I was on duty when she came back to the Hospital in a critical condition. She arrived gasping. We did advanced life support for her but she died shortly after.

From that sad day onwards, I wanted to be a dedicated family planning specialist helping women at most need. I couldn't remember not wanting to be an advocate for reproductive health rights.

It is my strong believe that this fellowship will broaden my knowledge and strengthen my professional experience in family planning.

December 17, 2019 was a historic day for Samuel. It was a day on which he finally applied for family planning fellowship training at St. Michael University Hospital. From the time he was a general practitioner all the way up his obstetrics and gynaecology residency training, no situation had made him change his mind.

Summarized in his motivation letter, the tragic loss of a young woman in his hands had remained a rubberstamp in his mind. To live had become for him to suffer from the pain of her death and saving other women from becoming victims of unsafe abortion was the only meaning he found in that suffering. For seven years, he had badly wanted to become only and only one thing - an expert family planning specialist.

Six candidates from different Hospitals across Ethiopia, none of whom he closely knew, were in competition with him to join the training program. He believed that he was going to make it, win in registering for the fellowship program and catch his dream of becoming a global reproductive health rights advocate. But, it was only his belief.

The decision to let him be who he wanted to be was largely in the hands of his examiners. His credentials represented only a small percentage of his likelihood of securing the place. His schedule to sit for the fellowship entrance interview was only a week away.

CHAPTER THREE

Samuel checked time. Sharp 10:00 AM. The weather in Addis Ababa was wet. There was a light rain. The temperature on weather forecast was 5 °C.

All faculty members of the department of obstetrics and gynaecology at St. Michael's Hospital were busy. Some of them doing ward rounds. Some of them doing ultrasound scanning. The rest were with undergraduate students doing Bedside teachings.

Samuel was there waiting for the interview at the department office along with the other six candidates, who were vying with him to procure the post-graduate training. A difficult race ahead. Only one out of seven of them was going to be selected.

He appeared to be in a good shape of preparation. He had a ready-made answer to the expected questions that could arise during the interview.

He knew it well. Always the unexpected happens. Samuel's hesitation was about the status of his knowledge about the unexpected questions that may come forward.

In the middle of his figuring out of what his interview might look like, one professor called him from the inside of the interview room. Time was up for his turn. He had no sympathetic stimulation. His body was in a complete state of calm.

He shove steadly into the room. He had radiant look. His hair was in buzz cut. Clean shaven beard. He wore Tan suit on blue tie with white strip and a white shirt. The color of his suit was a good match to the color of his skin, which was dark brown. His foot was on white socks and Beckett Simonon Loafers with vegetable-tanned stacked leather heel. Sparkling sliver Montblanc watch hanged on his right arm.

"Good morning Doctor Samuel Teshome. Please have a sit!", professor Getachew welcomed him with his graceful voice. He was the program director of fellowship programs at St. Michael's University Hospital.

"Pleased to have you on our interview. I am Professor Margot, chief of family planning division at Washington University", a female professor greeted him from the left side, before he sat down on the desk chair.

"Good morning! Thank you!", he reacted.

"Are you ready? Shall we start?", professor Getachew tested his readiness.

"Yes! You can.", he replied.

"Tell us about yourself.", the professor proceeded.

"I am 35 years-old, married and a father of two children. I am an assistant professor of obstetrics and gynaecology at St. Michael's University Hospital. I completed both my undergraduate and post-graduate specialty training at the same university where I am working at currently. I was born and grew up in Addis Ababa city. I completed my high school at Medhanialem Secondary School. I am interested in the practice of family planning and doing a clinical research."

"Great. Samuel, what is your strength and what is your weakness?"

"My strength is perseverance. My weakness is working with plan A only. I hate plan B."

"What are your expectations from this fellowship program.", Professor Margot leaned in.

"My greatest expectation is that it will empower me to become a competent clinician, trainer, researcher, leader in family planning."

"Why is family planning practice important to you?"

"Because it is a reproductive health right. It is a human right. Empowering women to have more control of their body is not a preference, rather a mandatory prerequisite to transform a society. It has been my dream to become an advocate of reproductive health rights for many years, since I was a general practitioner. I believe that this family planning fellowship program is the right place to personify my ambition."

"Okay Samuel. We have finished here. Have a good day!", the examiners said in unison. Samuel left the interview room in a cheerful mood.

Throughout the interview, he was with his composure. Whether his answers would be right or wrong, whether he would pass the interview and register for the fellowship program or not, it was a whole different story. The other candidates who waited for their turn to arrive could perform better than him.

As he anticipated, the interview was dominated by unexpected questions. None of it touched his motivation letter. None of it discovered his publication list. Samuel would remain in a week of unknown status about the result of his performance in the interview.

CHAPTER FOUR

Cheers and applause dominated a ceremonial Hall at Harmony Hotel. Hand clamps, whistles, shouting, screams, dancing, audience in the hall spared no means of celebrating the occasion.

Most of them were Ethiopians and seemed to have lost control of themselves. That included the guest of honor, mayor of Addis Ababa city. There was no even order of doing things. The mayor's security team was also dissolved in an ecstatic mood.

The whole crowd looked like football fans who broke into the pitch in celebration of a championship. They had pleasant host of reasons.

It was New Year eve. Exactly, midnight. Twenty-twenty was welcomed. Ethiopian Meron Asefa was pronounced Miss- Africa 2019, besting Herimela from Eritrea and

Germane from Rwanda at Harmony Hotel, a 5-star aspiring Hotel located in the heart of the commercial and entertainment district of Addis Ababa - Bole district.

The night was colorful. The inside perimeter of the hall was artfully dressed in a floor to ceiling red and white curtains. Lights in multiple color shinned from every corner. The dazzling light system reminded Rwandans in the hall of their Convention Center in Kigali at night. Creamy red hallway. Matching carpet. Beautifully decorated Christmas tree stood at the lobby of the Hotel.

Jovani was among Eritreans attending the event. He was there as an honorary guest on a business basis. He was introduced as the designer who helped Meron edge her success with his outstandingly designed dress of pure talent.

Ordinary style but extraordinarily designed Habesha skirt on a color-matched high-heeled shoes. His products seemed to represent, at least, a quarter of the beauty of the Miss Africa 2019. Beautiful introduction into the night and the year.

His name became as famous as Miss Africa 2019 at unbelievable speed. Nominated as best designer of the beauty race, he took it as a sign that 2020 was going to be his year.

Among his fortunes during the night was a ten thousand dollars award in recognition of his contribution in pushing the miss-Africa 2019 towards championship.

His business associates – one female and one male were at the event. They were too in a business tour. He had given them an assignment.

Meron worked as a model in his design company for two years. Jovani was the one who told her that she would be a star one day through hard work and self-belief. Up on remembering the day she joined his company, he understood very well every human being has a potential to shine out. Meron had become a living example for him that no independent person was born independent. He knew how much she lacked initially and how far she had prospered finally.

"Meron! Meron! Meron!" The whole crowd shouted her name aloud and it was broadcasted live on Ethiopia Television. She won 100,000 USDs award.

Instantly, he wanted to lay her off. He no more considered Meron's future in his design company as a model. Nor was she interested to represent his products anymore. If she was going to make it, she would divorce from her appointment at his business firm. They had agreed on it, days before the beauty contest.

She had made it and she was not a dependent person anymore. Jovani realized that it was time to give other women an opportunity to exploit the opportunities in his design business. He was looking for a replacement for her and his associates were given that specific assignment, to carry it out in the night and at the same place.

A matter of luck, the associates met two young ladies at the back in the ceremonial hall. After a brief exchange of talks with them, they confirmed the women's interest in modelling.

Moments later, they returned to their boss with fresh photos of the new ladies. The women were there to welcome the New Year and attend the beauty contest at the same time.

Jovani took a look at their photos. He liked them both. “I need to see them in person now.”, he demanded.

“Yes sir! Done! They are already in the Hotel’s lobby! Can I lead you, boss?”, one of his associates, the female one, responded.

“Fantastic! You guys are incredible!”, Jovani acknowledged his agents.

“Really?”, the second associate asked him.

“All the time!”, approved Jovani. He rapidly cross-checked the appearance of the women on photo against the reality on the ground, as he met them at the lobby. His female agent went ahead with a brief introduction.

“Hi! You already know him, best designer! Jovani, the legend of the night only preceded by Miss Africa herself!”

“Jovani, these are our newly selected potential upcoming models. Martha on the right and Birhan on the left.”

“Another blessing of the night! Look at them! Potential contenders of Miss Africa for the coming year.”, entertained Jovani.

“We have exchanged contacts. We have discovered that they are interested in modeling. We didn’t meet these women by a magic.”, the female agent claimed.

“I have told you. You guys are incredible but with hard work! I am sure, we will have the details later. Time to pay attention to their gifts.”, he sealed the agents claim.

“How old are you ladies?”, he opened a new dialog.

“I am 26 years-old!”, Birhan reacted first.

"I am 24 years-old!", Martha followed her.

"Oh my God! Take a look at them! Born rich are them!", he continued.

"Who are we without them?", his male agent inquired.

"Born to appreciate the born rich!"

"And whom are we going to grow in to with either of these new pearls of Red Sea added?"

"The taste of a cake gets better as you bite towards the inside of it. I can't believe that they are Eritreans - my sisters.", he wondered.

"Boss, who are we going to grow in to with either of these pluses?", the male agent reproduced his question.

"Climb towards Miss Universe claim!", retorted Jovani. "Well said, boss!", the male agent underlined.

"All the time!", the female agent agreed.

"So, when are we supposed to contact you again for the details of our hiring program?", Birhan questioned the female agent.

"We are going to give you a call on Monday, six days later. Either of you will sit for the job interview, a standard procedure we do before hiring new models. We will decide who over the weekends."

"Alright! Thank you very much for your interest in me and my friend. It would be a great honor to be working with you.", Martha expressed her appreciation representing herself and her friend.

“See you ladies next time. Good night”, said Jovani and disappeared into the pool party that was prepared to color the beauty pageant.

“We respect your interest to join us. Our company’s car is outside. The chauffeur can drive you home.”, the female agent requested to give them a ride.

“It is okay. We are taking a RIDE taxi lift.”, said Martha. Time was already 30 minutes past midnight.

CHAPTER FIVE

The sun was in Birhan's eyes. It blazed from the floor to floor glass windows of Shoa Mall that stood erect in front of her way. Monday was almost half in. Exactly, 11:55 AM. She darted across the street in-between Harmony Hotel and Best Western Plus Addis Ababa Hotel, from the left side of it.

She climbed up a single flight of stairs before she met the entry door to the mall. With her speedy pace, she was 10 minutes late. She had no time to admire the fabulous architect of the building that erected to a height of 100 feet. Windows in back color on white background color of the walls of building. Dust free spectacular staircases. High speed lifts. Flooded with hundreds of customers but no awful marketing buzz. Upper-class shopping center. There seemed no ordinary product for sale in the mall. And if there was any, it was at almost twice of the price in the ordinary markets in the city.

Birhan read ZARA FASHION CENTER few meters away in front of her, at the ground floor of the mall, as a female usher checked her body and purse for any arm possession. A decorated Christmas tree of medium size and a tall male toy stood to her left.

She flipped over one time and snatched her purse from the hands of the usher, once she was done with the checking. She needed to hurry up. She hastened towards the inside of the floor. She didn't catch any breath.

"Hello! Nice to see you again!". It was Sofia, Jovani's female associate, who greeted her at the doorway of the fashion center.

"I am so sorry for being late. Rash hour. You know the traffic jam in Addis. Thank you by the way."

"My pleasure. Relax. You are not late. My boss seems to have no deadline for you. I think you entered his business heart by a miracle. Few minutes back, I told him that you were late. Do you know what he said?"

"What?"

"March for a year if it is the way for your good health. He made it clear that he doesn't want to lose you at any cost. Please, take a seat!", she invited her to sit on the sofa of the reception room. Right away Birhan sunk into the comfort seat.

Sofia disappeared into the main store calling out, "Boss! She is here! The best Red Sea pearl is here."

"I am coming!", Jovani's echoed from the rear of the store of the fashion center.

Birhan sent her eyes to observe the traditional garments hanging on the walls of the center and contained in a

100% transparent glass boxes. The 6 meters by 6 meters showroom, which was face-to-face with the reception room, looked more like a museum than a business center. She had no enough time however to fully value all the awesome fashion and traditional clothes on display in the showroom.

"Signorina! Bon Rivato! Another beautiful day. Look at her. Cappuccino or tea? What do you like to have? I know. Long ride. The sun is burning outside. Would you like to have a cold drink?", Jovani saluted Birhan with his garrulous speech.

He was on super clean dirty Jeans trousers with black body T- shirt. He wore Sipriks Light Brown Wingtip dress shoes. He had a fresh haircut. He had a typical businessman's hair style with matching chin curtain facial hair style.

He also wore businessman's smile. Born to an Italian father and an Eritrean mother, Jovani owned an Arab look. His skin color was light brown.

"Hi! I am sorry for being late. I am fine with a glass of water.", Birhan responded. She swiftly scanned his handsomeness, as they shook in hands.

"Never mind. We are glad to have you here. I don't care how late. Well-come to Zara Fashion center.", said Jovani. He straight away plopped down on the sofa, right next to her.

"Thank you!"

"You are from Asmara. Right? Which neighborhood?"

"Geza Banda Tilian."

"Geza Banda! My favorite neighborhood. I grew up

visiting my uncle-Senor Eso, who lived up there even though I was based with my family at Tiravello."

"Really?"

"Ya! Princess from Geza banda. Hahahaha…Let's have lunch upstairs. I am sure we have a lot to tell each other." He terminated the conversation. She was in no position to reject his lunch invitation. She was in a business trip.

CHAPTER SIX

Sole e Luna Italian Restaurant, stationed on the first floor of Shoa Mall, was the best pizza house in the city. Nobody could tell that better than Jovani who was already there with Birhan at 30 minutes past noon, when the flow of customers to the restaurant peaked. Jovani prefered the Brenda area of the restaurant, which was quiet and empty, to be the place of their seat. He chose to talk to Birhan in privacy.

He pulled an armchair for her and himself. They sat face- to- face, an oval dining table in-between. Some of the customers causally greeted and congratulated him. Six days gone, Jovani was in his first week of celebration for his recent best designer nomination.

He took a closer look at her for a third time. He didn't name her princess out of the blue. She was gifted from top to bottom. The exact kind of hirable model he pictured in his mind.

It wasn't her wraparound blue dress with white strips. It wasn't from the low Gladiator high-heeled shoes. Birhan had a natural beauty. Curly and long hair. Darting thick lips on pink lipstick. Brown eyes. Dimpled chicks. Chocolate skin color. Glamorous and tall. He found her more than fit to show case his products.

"I hope you liked the restaurant.", he broke the seconds of silence between them. Birhan was shy to respond fast. Eager to win in her business trip, she didn't want her shyness to be discovered.

"Definitely. It is a gorgeous place. Everything in the mall looks a product of smart engineering.", she admitted the undeniable attractiveness of the restaurant.

"I brought you here to remind you of the pizza houses in Asmara back in the old good days. This is the best pizza house in Addis."

She smiled and nodded her head. He took it a sign that she had fully welcomed his preference.

"Two Margherita Pizza!", he ordered the humble female waitress who emerged with her appetite-opening look. She was dressed in white uniform with blue strips and on Sandal shoes.

"Back to business, I need to hear something about your background. I have your age and your measurement.", he initiated an informal job interview in a friendly way.

"I live her with my friend at Lafto neighborhood. I came to this country two years back. I won the 2016 DV lottery. I was late to cross the Ethio-Eritrea border illegally and…"

"Really sad!"

“I was late dealing with smugglers to make my arrival here safe. My DV lottery expired.”

“Oh My God! I am so sorry to hear this.”

“It is okay. I also tried to make it to Europe but that too failed.”

“A second bad luck. You are a strong woman. There is a third, fourth, etc chance in life. You will get another one. The best is yet to come.”

“Ya! I survived both losses and decided to lead my life here. I worked as a Manager at Alem Supermarket for the past two months.”

“Any other job?”

“I am a high school dropout. I used to do modeling. I participated at the Miss Eritrea beauty contest in 2014 and ranked at a third place.”

“Congratulations! As of today, you are hired as a model for our center.”, Jovani delivered the good news to her.

“Mr. Jovani! Thank you very much! I can’t believe this! May God bless you abundantly? I am lucky to be appointed at your center.”, she praised him as she suddenly noticed the awesome smell of the two Pizzas stretched on the dining table, which was ready for consumption. Her appetite was as full as it had never been.

Birhan couldn’t control her happiness. Finally, she got what she wanted. Doing modelling in Ethiopia had been in her mind for almost two years. January 6, 2020 came in with an opportunity of her desire.

"Mangi Birhan!", Jovani invited her to send her hands towards the table and enjoy the pizza.

"Okay!", she obeyed.

CHAPTER SEVEN

Sweet and busy January for Birhan and Jovani. He hired her as a model for 10,000-birr monthly salary and his fashion business boomed within a short period of time. Every design of dress advertised on Birhan's body turned favorite fashion dress of almost every young Habesha woman in Addis Ababa over a week time.

What he told her during their first face-to-face talk over lunch was actually taking place. He promised her that the best was yet to come for her. For the first time, she had found her life in Ethiopia meaningful. She moved to *Gerji condominium*, a residence apartment in the eastern side of the city, which is of better quality, freedom, and safety, in comparison to her previous house-rent. She was able to afford city life at a relatively expensive neighborhood in Addis.

The month passed with multiple schedules of business promotion. Jovani had seen the importance of opening branches of his fashion design company outside Addis-Ababa. He selected Shire town to be the site for the first branch of his business outside the capital.

The princess of Geza Banda Tilian and her boss had just arrived at MESOB INTERNATIONAL RESORT in Shire town. Present at the resort were also Sofia, other beauty contestants, and hundreds of audiences from the town. Traditional hut-like marble stone walled hotel rooms with its doors facing a beautiful lake, some twenty meters away. Big circus hall, cinema room, and classy Full-Service Restaurant Dining. Panoramic indoor pool and 90 square meters quiet area with panoramic views of wellness park behind the restaurant. Free internet access with Wi-Fi, 24-hour access gym, and Bootcamp spas. Mesob Resort had almost everything a vacationer would want.

Close to 7:00 PM. The fashion show hadn't begun yet. Off- stage, Birhan was on a cold shoulder strappy short sleeve party bodycon. It was white in color and designed with Ethiopian traditional material. Her foot was nested in Wedge Sandal shoes, which looked like an elbow junction with shining super sexy calf muscles distal to it and a proximal well aligned foot toes. Her lips were painted in Stella Rosae lipstick. She was very alert. No sign of tiredness.

Two hours back she was on board on Ethiopian Airline flight- ET-4536, from Addis Ababa to Shire. She and her designer travelled there to participate in Miss Ethiopia 2020 Beauty Pageant and inaugurate the first Zara Fashion branch outside Addis. The beauty contest event at the resort came first.

"Good evening our distinguished guests and beauty contest fans. Join me in welcoming the evening's contestants to the stage. First, Meron Ghirmay.", announced a female speaker dressed in white Habesha gown with braided hair, from the long T-shaped podium at the circus hall which was fully lighted.

In fraction of seconds, a five-foot-tall chocolate colored beauty contender appeared on stage. To the astonishment of Jovani and the evening's amusement, she was Birhan, the glamorous one-month old Model at Zara Fashion Center.

Her shinning appearance was a common sense for everybody in the superbly decorated meeting hall. The only difference and unique feeling that belonged to Jovani was that he picked the wrong articulation of her name. Birhan was pronounced as Meron.

The whole crowd applauded her. She was on a different level of prettiness. He became so impressed by her look that he decided to neglect his worry about how the rest of the crowd pronounced her name. His focus now was on her gifts now. He felt seduced.

Birhan wined up her show as other models on different designs of dress occupied the stage, turn by turn. Jovani seemed not to notice it.

Through his thought, she and her look waved constantly before his eyes. He remained so until the winners of the fashion show were revealed.

Birhan ranked at 1st place and won 100,000-birr award. The whole crowd cheered her win. His assessment, earlier, on New Year eve was right. Another star was born on that day. With her win in the fashion show, she just started to fully manifest her gifts and talent. He hurried to meet her in the backstage.

“Congratulation! I am more than happy. Wonderful start. Both for you and our branch in Shire. Princess of Geza Banda. Now, you have become also Princess of Shire town.”, he cheered her and gave her a light hug.

“Thank you, my boss. It was I guess for the type of dress you designed, and I shinned on it.”

“Bellissima! You are a smart addition to our center.”

“Thank you again”

“My honor and pleasure. I would like to host you dinner at this restaurant this evening and for the wonderful job that you did, it may sound premature, but I have reached at a decision to promote you to become the General manager at our center in Addis. One of the associates will be moved to this town.”.

She had to trust him. What he told her so far about her future had turned out to be real. What a great start for her! Birhan climbed into the position of claiming one hundred thousand birr and a job promotion at the same time. She used to hear that magic works for some people. She was there, one of those people. In her mind, she played Drack’s best song– ‘God’s plan’.

“Why did the announcer miss your name? Had she lost her mind?”, Jovani asked her up on their entry into the resort’s restaurant.

“I am sorry! I didn’t tell you but my official name is Meron Ghirmay. Birhan is a name given to me by my mother. I grew up named Birhan in my neighborhood and anywhere out of school. Be it here or back home many people know me as Birhan.", she answered.

"How did the announcer come to discover what I didn't in one month?", he questioned her again.

"There was a mandatory registration of names before we showed up on stage. The person saw my official name on my identity card."

"And then?"

"For certification purpose in witness of my participation in the fashion show, he preferred that official name, he asked me permission though. And that was how I was introduced to the stage as Meron."

"Ah Dio! How come it was skipped during your first registration as a model in our center?"

"Sofia asked me only about my father's name. I think she took it for granted that my official name was Birhan."

"You didn't tell her?"

"I didn't. I am commonly known as Birhan except, as I told you, at the place of headache- School. I like my second name very much."

"But I would like to call you by your first name - Meron! It sounds beautiful. I believe if you work hard you could grow to become miss-Africa next year."

"You are kidding right. Let me be fit enough to persist in your business first."

"You are more than fit now. Meron I like your smile. I guess you look also beautiful when you cry. I don't believe that your beauty could fade with situations."

"Thank you! You are crediting me beyond what I deserve. I think the situation is becoming about being from the city- our Asmara."

"No. I am serious. Don't get me wrong. I am lucky to exploit your potential before any other designer in this country."

Time ran close to midnight. Two hours passed since they had dinner. They were still together at the restaurant and the taste of the mouth-watering fried chicken dinner dish was fresh in their tongues. Their post-dinner chat, accompanied by a cocktail, covered their past lives, including each other's sexual life.

"It may sound a little stubborn to ask you this question. Because you are now not only a model at my business firm but my sister. Would you mind?", said Jovani and their talk grew more serious.

"Don't worry at all. I will only forward you the answers. Just try me.", Meron reassured him.

"Are you in a relationship?", Jovani proceeded.

"Oh! Nope! I am still single."

"No boyfriend?"

"Many years back I had one but situations changed. I have been single for the last four years. Are you?", she asked him back.

"It has been a year since I broke-up my long-term girlfriend. I walked for four years in that relationship but you are right situations change. Here I am single."

"What time is it? I think it is getting late. I am sorry but I feel tired. I got to walk to my room.", she suddenly withdrew from their private chat and paraded few steps before she flipped to say goodbye to him. She was right. It was 30 minutes past midnight.

"Bona neti! Good night beautiful! Your room is near by. I don't think you would need my accompany.", he hinted.

"Absolutely right!", she underscored and left the restaurant.

Meron counted one hour in her hotel room at the resort. Still, she couldn't fall asleep. Unsettled emotional dust filled her brain. She tried different methods to distract the attention of her brain. She tried to watch TV program. She put off the light and closed her eyes. She took warm and descent bath. All the luxury and the silence in the room couldn't help her fall to sleep.

It wasn't her first time to be in Shire town. She had lived there for two years. She relived the disturbing moment in her life that forced her to abandon the town. She recollected everything about that moment exactly as it happened, and as if it occurred a day ago.

CHAPTER EIGHT

A bright November morning in 2019. The sun was up and its rays illuminated well the whole Shire town. Shire, a bustling and green town in Tigray (northern Ethiopia region) was at its best season to be visited by tourists.

Thanksgiving light wind blew from the farmlands at the outskirts of the town towards the down-town, carrying clean air along with it. The pavements of the streets of the town was packed with crowd who marched up and down. Private and state-owned enterprises were active. *Silassie Church* sat at a hillside that camped the town on the western side. It was a magnificent view that Meron couldn't enjoy fully through the window of her Hotel room. Her memories of a night before masked her from sighting the beauty of the town with concentration.

She didn't know immediately how and why but she was there at Denait Hotel, a five-story poorly designed architect painted in yellow color that stood at the center of a busy marketplace.

She checked time on her Nokia mobile with a blurred vision. It was 10:30 AM. Again, she didn't know how but an ugly smell filled her breath. She was vomiting an hour ago. Her anger galvanized as she recounted what went wrong in her life on Friday night, the night before. As far as she could remember, first she entered a strange bar -Bar Shenen -on the right side of a narrow cobble stone street, close to Hayelom Statue. She arrived there early, 30 minutes before her appointment time.

Tigrigna music in the bar went hot as time went close to 7:30PM. Male customers who looked in their late 30s started to dance to it. The new person that she was introduced through her friend-Dejen, hadn't showed-up yet. She waited for an hour and she didn't want to stay beyond that. Her calculation was that the person was minding another business. She could have made a phone call to him- she had his number. But it wouldn't make any difference. She was sure that he could not forget their appointment under any circumstance.

Meron felt embarrassed as she discovered that she was the only female customer in that male-dominated inner-city bar. An idea of leaving the bar revolved around in her brain. Before she transformed her thought into an action, she observed a black man, who looked like in his early forties, marching towards where she was located.

The man had eyes in brown color like hers and he wore twists hair style. He was on black dirty jeans and turtleneck sweater. Figaro gold chain hanged on his left arm. His Brogue shoes were polished and gleaming in the dim light of the bar but it was more noticeable for the crunch noise it created, as he stepped faster towards Meron.

"Nice to meet you Meron. I am John again.", he reintroduced himself to her before he grabbed a chair and joined her.

"Nice to meet you too.", she responded.

"What shall I bring you?", a young woman dressed in black uniform requested them. She showed up before they went deep into their conversation.

"A unit Whisky for me and for her… Meron, what do you like to have?", John hastily ticked his preference.

"A bottle of sprite would suffice!", Meron breathed out. She was shy to shoot a full look at him.

"Do you know why I preferred this bar to be our place of meeting?", he reentered their conversation.

"Sorry, I don't."

"It is a hidden bar, away from the downtown, we can fully secure our privacy to discuss on the deal."

"Still, I don't fully understand."

"A secret possessed by one person goes to the graveyard when he or she dies. A secret that two people share lives without a local spread. A secret shared by three people is not a secret anymore- before they notice it, it will be widespread."

"Wise words indeed."

"You know security agents in this country have hyper sensible ears. What we do has to remain a secret between me and you."

“Have my word. It will remain a secret.”

“You look a smart girl. You don’t only look but you are, actually.”, John admired her while he gulped the unit of whisky in his right hand down.

“Let me start with the payment. You are expected to pay 6,000 dollars. It is a three-stop route. A second unit please!”, he interrupted his chase of the deal and ordered the waitress to bring him a second unit of whisky. The waitress didn’t take time to pour additional unit of his favorite fuel into his empty glass.

“You will travel to Sudan from here guided by an expert. Then, you will be welcomed by our agents in Khartoum and stay there for one month. Next, you will penetrate the Sahara Desert to arrive at Tripoli, Libya. A boat will be ready for you within a week of your arrival there and take you finally to Italy.”, he cut short into the chase.

“I am sorry. You are amazing. Had I had 6,000 USDs, I wouldn’t bear an idea of moving out of this country in mind.”, Meron gave him a bitter answer. And it was very clear for him.

CHAPTER NINE

The whole MESOB INTERNATIONA RESORT was quiet. Only a sound of distant barking dogs could be heard. She noticed a knock on the door of her hotel room, amid her being absorbed in memory of her special Friday at Shire town. Terrified, she put the light on. Her fear or flight reaction to the scary knock turned on.

She erected her ears and her eyes were wide open. Her heartbeat became faster and lauder as if a drum bass was inserted in her chest. Her body started to shake.

"Who… who is it?", she stuttered.

"It is me. Jovani.", a masculine voice echoed.

"Wait! A moment please!", she urged him. Her body stopped shaking. She tiptoed towards the bathroom. She washed her face and dried it with a towel.

"Meron, surprise!", Jovani greeted her with a red rose, as she opened the door of the hotel room.

"I know it feels disgusting and weird to knock at your door in the middle of the night.", he quickly diverted his speech towards what brought him to her hotel room at 1:30 AM.

"It is okay. I was awake.", she replied.

"Meron! I have been pretending for the whole month. You have entered my heart from the moment I saw you at the Beauty contest on New Year eve. I am crazy in love with you. I have been consumed by your love. I don't know where to start. But now it is something that I cannot bear to carry on without sharing it to you. I have become so weak to keep it a secret. I want to be your friend and beyond. I have been attracted to your beauty, talent, brilliance, humbleness, everything. I want to be with you now and always. I stood behind the door of your hotel room for almost 40 minutes, figuring out how to tell you all this.", Jovani fully confessed about his fall in love with her.

"Oh my God! I don't know what to say! Can we go back to the restaurant and talk in depth?", Meron proposed.

She did like Jovani but she never imagined that he would show up at the doorstep of her hotel room, at the time when she needed someone to distract the attention of her brain. "Now you are the boss. What you say is right. Would you let me take a hold of your hands? Señorita! You are beautiful.", Jovani declared his surrender to her love.

"I want to listen why you love me in detail piece by piece before anything else.", said Meron. This time, it was her turn to interview him the way she liked to.

“Yes Shikorina! What else shall I obey you, my princess?”

“Wait a moment. I need to put on a jacket. Thank you!”, Meron suggested. She took the rose out of his hand and slammed the door of her hotel room closed. She smelled the pleasant odor of the rose. She felt as if she sniffed heroin powder. She felt more than a woman, on earth and beyond. She put the rose on her bed. In a moment, she put her jacket on and joined Jovani.

He took her hand in his as they paced together towards the elegant traditional restaurant. He was already given a green light to do that. Action speaks more than words. Meron turned her best ever smile on.

Only the casher and one waitress were there to receive their orders at the restaurant.

“Hello! What can I help you?”, a courteous waitress in blue uniform with braided hair received them with her meek voice, as soon as they located themselves at the right corner.

“Would you like to eat something?”, Jovani deferentially referred to Meron.

“No. Just Avocado juice.”, she replied.

“Two avocado juice.”, Jovani ordered.

“Why do you love me?”, Meron grilled him about the depth of his love for her.

“Because you are such a lovable person.” “What?”

“I am kidding.”

“Why are you kidding? I am serious.”

"Because, I love you."

"Okay let me cut it short. What do you really want from me?"

"Beautiful baby!"

"Are you sleepy?"

"Not really but hypnotized by your alluring smile and shape of your body."

"What kind of life do you imagine living with me?"

"You mean that I desire to live?"

"Whatever and however you want to put it."

"A happy life. Create beautiful family. Walk to the heaven's door through the peace that you and I and our children create together. Meron, I love you with all my heart. Do you?"

She brought her face closer to his and sent her lips to kiss him. They huddled in love and they seemed inseparable. They were in the tightest hug imaginable.

"My room or your room?", he whispered into her ears.

"Take me in your hands. Whatsoever.", she hinted him. In two minutes, they were in his room, naked wrapping around each other's body on bed. He stared at her eyes, the center of her gravidity that pulled any man who took a closer look at it.

Dimpled chicks allayed with beautifully arranged white teeth fitted in sockets of black gums, Meron owned a smile that could heal a soul.

She held him tighter in her brace and felt a hard massage of his well-built biceps and pictorials on her breast. Naked, Jovani – the businessman- looked like a body builder. At the age of 33 years-old, he owned the type of body that any woman would love.

"I love you with all my heart", her verbal answer to Jovani's critical question arrived lately.

"I love you too.", he sighed. Their night became full of light. They signed to become one. Not on a piece of paper but a physical one – they made love. An outstanding start. A foundation stone for their awesome journey of having a happy life was laid then.

CHAPTER TEN

There have now been more cases of the novel coronavirus outside of mainland China than inside, according to numbers from the World Health Organization. While China, the early epicenter of the outbreak, has still had more confirmed cases than any other country – more than 80,000 –a number of other countries have surged in recent days, including Italy with more than 24,000 cases, Iran with almost 14,000 and Spain with more than 7,000.

On February 26, the World Health Organization reported for the first time that the majority of new cases per day had come from outside of China. This trend has continued as newly confirmed cases in China have dwindled in recent days, while other countries have

> *discovered thousands of new infections – including the United States, which has now reported more than 3,000 cases.*

Meron followed March 15th CNN Television breaking news, from a new house at Sarbiet Neighborhood, through a widow of a 55-inch smart SAMSUNG TV. Built on 500 square meters area, the house was a modern villa with five bedrooms, big salon room, a kitchen, and two bath rooms.

It had been one month since she mingled with Jovani and started living together with him at his luxury villa. But he wasn't there with her at the time when a new milestone was reached about the corona pandemic.

The whole world was feeling the shadow of the hundreds of thousands of people's lives that would be lost due to the pandemic, in a span of three months that followed.

Like any other of citizen of world, Meron had the panic attack of the virus incubated in her gut. Still, there was no widespread disease in Ethiopia. Clouds of fear of spikes of infection had already arrived in the sky of the capital Addis Ababa.

The threat of the COVID-19 infection had spread across the globe like a wildfire and everybody was being affected. Residents of Addis Ababa felt they were not going to be an exception.

The price of mask, hand sanitizer, and 95% alcohol had sky- rocketed in the city, which had reported its first case of COVID-19 only 48 hours back.

Jovani and Meron had spent an enjoyable six weeks of romance, before the pandemic. They partied together at different high-rank clubs in Addis. They often passed a pleasant time at luxurious bars at the city. They toured many resorts across Ethiopia. Abundantly blessed, Meron's life went from meaningful to complete. She received the most romantic proposal from him. She said, "yes" to it.

But the corona pandemic disrupted everybody's life. Their fashion design business dwindled; the number of customers was on a decline. She was there alone given the responsibility of running it. Her fiancé, her dream love, was away in Rome. He travelled to corona hard hit Italy two weeks back. He was told that his father, Lazeroo, turned COVID-19 positive and was critically ill admitted to a Hospital.

Following his wife's tragic death in 2014 in a car accident in Asmara, Lazeroo completely moved to Rome to pass his remaining age with his only daughter – Angela (Jovani's elder sister). He hadn't gone back to Asmara ever since. Jovani followed his father's move to Italy initially but later changed his mind to open a business, a fashion center, in Ethiopia.

Addis Ababa was not in any form of lockdown at the time the beginning of the pandemic but nobody knew what lied in the horizon. The guess at large was the city would follow Cape Town, another big city in Africa that had already fall under complete shutdown.

Meron had additional problem that kept her worried. It was her irregular menses. She had the problem for 11years since her menarche. It shouldn't be a big concern for her then. She could have post- phoned her medical visit. But, until when? The wave of the corona virus infection didn't seem to pass soon.

With the breaking CNN news that she followed in the night of March 15, she was very much sure that it wouldn't be over in a month or two. She remained in touch with Jovani across a phone call. There was no hope that he was coming back soon. Her destined father-in-law, Lazeroo was in ICU, admitted with a diagnosis of severe COVID-19 disease.

She was lucky to have met Lazeroo, the most jovial father she had ever known next to her own father. She had the opportunity to chat with him but across a telephone call. Right, before he became critically sick. She loved his welcoming of her. He fully embraced her as the destined wife of his youngest son. They adored talking to each other very much though it didn't last long.

Agony tore through her as the health of her forthcoming father-in-law became endangered. She was scared that she might lose every good deed that she had come to build with Jovani. It was highly likely that he could pass away. And in the worst case scenario, Jovani could contract the disease and become disconnected from her forever. He was at the epicenter of corona virus infection.

Corona virus crisis is a reality predicted in a science fiction story-The contagion Movie. It was an opinion of many, including Movie-mad Meron. She spent her evening a day before watching the movie on Television Screen at the big salon room. Fact Vs. fiction. The only difference she analyzed was in the names of the viruses. COVID-19 was the real and unknown virus in the science fiction.

She replayed all the scenes of the movie in her brain, as early as she got out of bed, next morning. She was deadly sure that the crisis of the pandemic was only in the beginning across the world.

Spiking reports of the deadly viral infection from around the world. Cities around the world in lockdown. Supermarkets running out of store. What was narrated as a fiction in the science fiction movie was already happening in 2020.

'What a Posthumous work! There is no fiction story in this world. Only a matter of time until it becomes real.' Meron asserted as she finished washing her face, before she moved out of the master bathroom. She sat around a wooden dining table for breakfast and further argued with herself that the science fiction story must have been written by an extra-ordinary writer, an intelligence agent or a prophet. Time was already 8:00 AM.

If the virus was a conspiracy, as it was believed to be so by many, she was definitely correct that it was a classified intelligence document that leaked as a fiction. It would mark the dooms day if the writer of the science fiction was a prophet according to her belief at that time.

She didn't know but the morning she woke up into with flashbacks of the science fiction movie would mark the beginning of the materialization of the prophecy of her own life.

Menstrual irregularity, her immediate concern at that time was like a show room to what the future held for her. To address her problem, she had made-up her mind to make a visit to a clinic. She had to take her menstrual irregularity seriously.

Her decision didn't lack information. She spent the rest of the day at home thinking over it and shared it to Sofia later on. Sofia was her magic bullet every time she needed help. At the age of 35 years-old and being 9 years older than Meron, she knew a lot about problems that belonged to women only. She approved Meron's decision to make a visit to a clinic. The situation of the corona infection could get worse in the country, specifically in the capital Addis.

"Check yourself girl. Take it seriously. At the age of 26, the irregularly of your menstrual period should improve not get worse. It could be pregnancy", Sofia had warned her, minutes before she went to sleep during that night. And that was a message which she ought not to miss, in any case.

The norm for Meron was to see her menses sometimes every two months and sometimes after 45 days. This time, it was one month outside the norm. For the first time, her menses had gone unseen past two months. January 7 was the date on which she saw her last period.

She got up late the following morning. She ate her breakfast meal- himbasha with tea- quickly. Her plan for the day was to check herself in to the clinic before noon. Her 150 dollars-worth Casio G- Shock watch, a gift from Jovani, ticked thirty minutes past 10 AM. It was still cold outside. The whole city of Addis Ababa was blanketed with thick dark clouds. No need for weather forecast. It was easy to tell that it would soon start to rain. Meron didn't miss that.

She changed her pajamas fast and put on her high waist blue jeans, crop-top shirt and her black leather jacket which covered all her body except her face and lower extremities. She picked up her umbrella. And she was ready to leave.

CHAPTER ELEVEN

It took her Thirty minutes taxi ride to get from her home to Kidus Clinic in Mexico neighborhood. Soon it would be noon. The day was Sunday, the only day on which she had free time to deal with things out of fashion business, even though the business at their center had slowed down since the time Corona was declared pandemic by the WHO. She was there at the clinic to find an answer to the question why her period came late always and why it was beyond late for the first time. She had a suspicion at large that she could be pregnant.

The building of the clinic looked like a house with a large front yard. Painted in white color, the five rooms in it only served an OPD service with simple laboratory tests. It consisted of two examination rooms, a reception room, one laboratory room and a toilet.

Meron facilitated her card issuing and she was guided by a nurse in blue scrubs to one of the examination rooms. Her time was up and she quickly entered the room.

"Hi! What can I help you please?", the only attending physician at the clinic saluted her, seconds after she took a seat on a Shell chair, behind the Doctors table.

"Doctor! I didn't see my menses for the last three months.", Meron gave her answer.

"I am ordering urine test and pelvic ultrasound for you and we will discuss about your problem later! Oh! Sorry, we don't have ultrasound. You will take a prescription paper and do it outside- in near-by Maternity centers.", the physician rushed to order investigations for her.

'*Urine test, Why the hell not*' Meron spoke to herself. She would be more than happy if her result turned out to be positive.

Meron had unprotected sexual intercourse with Jovani multiple times, during the two months of their romance. She wouldn't get surprised if she turned to be pregnant. Her tiny hesitation was about the fact that the whole world was walking into a situation that was largely unknown. The fetal effects of corona virus infection was not well-studied at that time. Both of them badly wanted to create a beautiful family. If her pregnancy test turned positive, what Jovani said before they made their first love at Mesob Resort, was going to start to be fulfilled. '*Create beautiful family. Walk to the heaven's door through the peace that she and Jovani and their children create.'*

"Okay!", she nodded in agreement with the doctor's quest to order investigations for her. She left the examination room with a urine test and obstetric ultrasound request paper in her hand. She prayed to her God to bless her by turning her pregnancy test positive. That was what she wanted at the unprecedented time of the corona pandemic.

"Meron! You are pregnant!", Doctor Abel congratulated her before she took a sat. It had been an hour since Meron submitted urine specimen for pregnancy test.

She felt the run of high dose adrenaline in her blood stream. Her heart was gulping 'dup-lup, du-lup' at a rate it had never hit before. The breaking news about her being pregnant dissolved her face in tears of joy. It all happened in a fraction of a second.

"We need to see your ultrasound result that will help us to know everything, including how old your gestation might be.", he reminded her. She didn't seem interested to hear anything further. Her mind was busy celebrating the news. She pulled out her iPhone 8 cell phone from her pink Flight bag and searched Jovani's number. She dialed his number two times but the line was busy twice. She tried for a third time. This time it worked but Jovani didn't answer the call.

CHAPTER TWELVE

"**H**ello! Sofia, how are you? I need to talk to you urgently, can you meet me at Saliem café? Now?"

"Sure. Anything wrong?", Sofia asked Meron from the other end of a late afternoon phone call.

"Better to tell you in person.", Meron decided to quickly end the call.

Meron and Sofia had become very good friends. They looked as if they were life time friends in a short period of time. It took them only three months to believe in each other's sincerity, confidentiality, capacity, and flexibility. A reflection of this, Sofia was the only true friend Meron had whom to she could fully entrust with her everything. Good and bad. Right and wrong. Past and present.

For Sofia, Meron was among the few positive friends she ever had in her lifetime. It was her guess that, even this time, she needed her urgently for something positive. Meron never liked to bother her good friends whenever she faced a problem, unless it was a very concerning one. She wasn't like the kind of person who would love to complain every time he or she met a king.

Sofia didn't take time to see Meron at Saliem Café on the second floor at Shoa Mall. It took her only 30 minutes to reach there from her home at Gerji condominium.

"Hi! How is your day?", said Meron inviting Sofia to take a sit with her gesture. Quickly, she changed her gesture to an act of pulling a chair in respect of her good friend.

Sofia wore a red lipstick, which matched with her long coat that completely covered her light green Sheath dress. She was on Mary Jane shoes. Tall in height, with her hair in face- framing layers, she had the look of Duchess Kate at Christmas services with the royal family except the light black color of her skin, her broad nose, and her thick lips.

"Thank you, my friend! I happy to be here with you. Do you know why am I happy?"

"I don't know. You tell me…Sofia."

"I am just seeing your face. Is there anything that makes me happier than this?"

"I know. You are likewise to me. That is why I needed you now in my time of adversity.", Meron geared the conversation towards revelation of her shocking news.

"What happened?"

"It is a tragedy…", sobbed Meron. She couldn't complete her sentence. Soon, rivulets of tear started to race down her both chicks. Sofia's shock heightened.

"I checked in a clinic today-Kidus Clinic, just two hours back. The physician told me that I am pregnant."

"Congratulations! A great blessing! Wow!"

"But it is a four months-old pregnancy.", Meron told her how her day turned upside down.

"You know it. Our relationship with Jovani is only two-months old. And I am carrying a four months old baby.", she detailed her further as she dried her eyes with a napkin.

"Take it easy! It could be by mistake.", Sofia tried to calm her down.

"It was a gynaecologist who examined me with ultrasound at another private Hospital. He said the margin of error is maximum only one week. It doesn't make any difference.", she argued back.

Sofia understood that Meron carried a pregnancy of mistaken paternity. She saw no need of confirmation. She knew the exact age of Meron's affair with Jovani.

"My life is devastated. I slept with another man four months back. Look at what Jovani has to say or do. I will never let him kiss a baby of stolen paternity.", Meron unfolded her long time keep secret. Her face became flooded with tears again. Her conjunctivae was on red injection.

"Trust me. Your life will never be devastated. Was he your boyfriend?", asked Sofia.

"Ya kind of. It was unhealthy relationship which didn't last beyond a nightstand. It was very brief. Now, I have its consequence. I am in the twilight of my future.", she gave her reply.

Meron remained speechless for two bad minutes. She looked like she had an absence seizure. Quite from outside but a great deal of distraction inside her brain. '*Body inside, mind outside*'. Beyond Salief café, her mind traveled hundreds of miles towards north of Ethiopia at a speed of light. It was at the mysterious Bar in Shire town. She revisited her traumatic experience at the town four months back. The scene in which John raised an irrelevant question clicked first in her mind. Then another scene. Then the other scene.

CHAPTER THIRTEEN

"Is it correct that girls dislike boys that only talk?", John asked Meron without shame. She was stunned. Within seconds, her stun turned into an annoyance, as he raised another irrelevant question.

"Would you like to drink Whiskey? It tastes good. Above all, it easily dries out stress, boredom, any bad feeling."

"No. I don't drink alcohol. Thank you!", she rejected his invitation.

"I know. Women act as if they don't like to drink alcohol. Pretend. Until when? Until you find the thing in your hand. Ahahaha…", John tried to extinguish her anger.

"Meron! Please one shot. You want me to drink alone? We are going to do something big together that is going to guarantee your future at a fair payment. I am making you a favor. I am going to reduce the price to 3000 dollars.", he implored her to drink Whiskey again.

"I am sorry but I don't want to drink any alcohol.", she dismissed his request for a second time. She didn't give any attention to his statement of cutting the price of smuggling her to Europe by a half.

"Okay! Cool!", John admitted his failure to influence her to consume alcohol. He smiled but it was a false one. Without shame, he sent his well-built right arm wrapping around her neck. He gave her a sexy squeeze. She became furious again but she didn't know how to make him behave in the noisy bar dominated by men, and she wasn't encouraged to immediately withdraw from the deal. She only swayed his arm with all her strength.

John knew how to exactly carry out his conspiracy with perfection. He believed that a thieve had to be intelligent enough not to rely on God but his ability to defend everything.

He quickly let her body go out of his brace. But he continued brewing his plot. Try something repeatedly but in different ways. It was his style in handling sensitive cases.

"Meron please taste it. It is a good mix to your sprite.", he begged her for a third time. They remained the only customers in the bar as time got close to 9:00 PM.

She had to walk back to her home in the Southern part of the town, before it was late. Against her will, she found herself stranded in the hot bar by a muscular smuggler who wanted to dominate her with his speech and masculine.

Effective strategy. He finally succeeded in pushing her towards alcohol ingestion. She complied, "Okay! Just only one shot. One unit. This is only to respect your invitation.", Meron suddenly changed her mind.

The waitress brought her a unit of Black-Level Whiskey. She tried it on her tongue. The taste was ugly. John observed her face frowning.

"Add the sprite in to it. It is going to taste wonderful.", he suggested rapidly. She did what he said. She consumed the unit of whiskey in four gulps.

"Back to business, there is a guy who is leaving a week later from this town. He will take you on a bus through Humera to Khartoum.", John reentered the chase and held his plot standstill while he ordered a second unit of whisky for her and a fourth one for himself. He thought it was important to kill time. And she couldn't say no to his order.

"I promise you that you will not pay more than 3000 USDs. You see, tone of speech matters. I just have cut 3000 USDs because of your good attitude.", he completed the chase. Soon he was going to begin his race for the plot from a standstill.

Moving to Sudan was the beginning of the illegally legal route of migration to Europe. Meron felt that finding the way of making it to Europe at a cheaper price was worth of complying with ingestion of a single shot of alcohol. She took her planned migration to Europe as a plan B sent to her from God.

Her DV lottery procession was her plan A, the reason that brought her in to making a decision of crossing to Ethiopia illegally. Her opportunity of making it to United States disappeared in the darkness of her late arrival in Ethiopia.

Non-consensually, John touched Meron over her chest. She was in the middle of ingesting the second unit of the alcoholic beverage.

"This is ridiculous!", she thwarted his seduction with her aggressive response. She swayed his right arm for the second time.

He apologized, "I am so sorry. My hand goes before my tongue whenever I become attracted to beautiful women.".

John only needed to stretch time until the alcohol poured in to Meron's stomach find its way to be in her blood stream. He wanted to kill time by fabricating a long apology. He was right. His prediction about what would happen to Meron in the minutes that followed was going to work.

"*Aba shawil ziban cherhi, tewelia werhi*", Meron started to sing aloud the Tigrigna soundtrack that dominated the bar the whole evening. What it meant was obvious for him.

'*I told you, John you are a hero you can't fail.*' he praised himself. Yes, he did win at last. Drug-facilitated sexual assault worked for him with precision.

CHAPTER FOURTEEN

Meron felt a strong vibration in the palm of her left hand. Her iPhone was ringing. It woke her up from her dark memoires at the mysterious bar in Shire town four months ago. Her attention was brought forcefully back to Saliem Café. The caller was Jovani, her romantic gem. She brought her cell phone towards her left ear.

"Mio Amore! Come Stai!?" Jovani's voice came in.

"I am doing good darling. Not to mention how much I miss you. Are you safe Honey? Dooms day in Italy. How is our Dad doing? Is he getting better? Is he still under critical care? Here we are doing fine. The business is down but health wise, I am doing good. Sofia is also here with me.", she greeted him back.

"I am doing fine. Mio padre is still in the ICU. Don't worry about the business. We will rebuild it when I come back. As the world wishes, Corona will vanish by the end of April. I am praying honey to God to put Dad on a full recovery.", Jovani briefed her.

"Glad to hear that you are fine. I have been praying for our Dad for the last ten days."

"Bravo! Sempre bravo! It is a difficult time honey. But it will definitely get better."

"May God let it be!"

"Ya! We will get through this. It is our sins Honey. The world went out of control. Corruption. Genocide. Murder. Dictatorship. Systematic abuse. Gun violence. Racism. Rape. Our world has repeated the mistake that brought the old world in to a collapse. God is raising his flag that we have reached his intolerable limit.", the line went dead on Meron's end. Her cell phone was all of a sudden on a dead battery. She was pissed off.

"What happened? Is his father okay?", Sofia asked. She partially understood their conversation. She knew that Senor Lazeroo had turned COVID-19 positive.

"He said that he is very sick and is admitted to ICU.", Meron answered.

"My goodness! I am so sorry to hear this."

"What makes it worse is that Italy is under lockdown. And Jovani is not able to visit and take care of him."

"I know! It's major headlines on every news network. And we don't know when the lockdown is going to be over."

"God knows. Maybe it is until he says our punishment is over."

Sofia boosted what Jovani already said. He put it all into a religious perspective. He wasn't the first one though. Many people took the corona pandemic as if it was God's anger response. More than 10,000 deaths corona virus deaths were recorded in Italy on March 29. United States was steeping towards becoming the world epicenter of corona infection.

Meron refuted Jovani's statement. '*Where would corona find the evil doers? The dictators? The killers? The money grabbers? The rapists? The human traffickers?*', she disputed in her thought.

Without his knowledge, Jovani re-exposed her to her dark past in Shire town. Memories of her horrific night at the mysterious bar appeared in her brain for a third time.

"Look at these two women. They are not as beautiful as me. Not even close, with all the pride they have being in their homeland country.", Meron double-confirmed John her fall under the influence of alcohol. She jumped from singing of an abrupt onset to hailing her beauty with alcohol-induced double vision. Her voice was audible from everywhere with in the bar.

"I don't need anybody to tell me this truth about you. That's why I am here with you.", John groaned.

The wall clock in the bar rang 10:00 PM. Meron lost balance of everything. Her gait, speech, and vision became anomalous. She had become incapacitated. Wickedly, he had celebrated it. He only needed a private room to satisfy his sexual exploitation crave in privacy. Few minutes later, he took her to his Hotel room. And he non-consensually undressed her and forced himself into her. Born criminal, John had already booked a room at Denait Hotel. He was knowledgeable on how to fool the lady at the reception, as he returned to the hotel supporting drowsy Meron from her side.

CHAPTER FIFTEEN

"Four months-old pregnancy is not too late. There is a way to solve this. You can have safe abortion.", Sofia clued Meron.

Sofia's quick fix shook Meron and put her back to 2020. It erased the disturbing memories of her sexual abuse from her mind though temporarily. Suddenly, Meron became herself-the beautiful model filled with many ambitions.

"You are my trouble shooter Sofia. You were the first one who picked me up and put me in to this road of success-modeling. Here you are with me the first person running to extinguish the fire – the unintended pregnancy-blazing inside my womb.", Meron appreciated her friend's contribution in her life.

"Let's keep it a secret. It is good that Jovani is away in Italy. The only good news for you about this corona crisis.", Sofia reminded her not to get overstressed.

“What other option do I have?”, Meron asked her back.

“No option. Unintended pregnancy is like a Jealousy. Either it kills you or it makes you kill yourself.”

“How did you know this all. You look like a professional counselor?

“I was rapped at the age of 14 years-old. I got pregnant. I was mentally disturbed. I wanted to kill myself. I was not motivated to speak about it initially.”

“Why?”, Meron interrupted her.

“Because, it was my stepfather who sexually assaulted me. I was afraid to share it to anyone because the consequences were visible. The entire family was going to disintegrate with a bad name and shameful reputation. Later on, I told one of my friends and she helped me to access abortion care at a hospital in secret.”

“Oh! I am so sorry Sofia. You are a rape survivor? Hard to believe.”, Meron expressed her sympathy as if she had never been in her shoes.

“I was a high-school student at that time. I dropped out of school. Because, I couldn’t cope with the stress. I kept it a secret for long. It is a long story but I am cutting it short here. Promise to chat you more some other time.”

“You are a fighter Sofia. A strong woman. Nobody can see the struggle you have gone through, including me.”

“Thank you! Back to your problem. So, let’s make an arrangement. St. Mary clinic is the exact place to solve your problem at. Many of my friends had been treated there.”

“Alright. Thanks God! You saved my life. You put my heart back to its regular business. I was really depressed for the last four hours. I thought many things, including harming myself. Talking to you was the first and last thought I bore in my mind.”

“It is okay! It is my duty. I told you there is nothing that pleases me more than seeing your happy face. And now being able to help you makes me even happier. Let’s fix time. Shall we do it on the coming Monday? It is going to be your choice.”

“Okay! I will give you a call and let you know tomorrow.”

CHAPTER SIXTEEN

Meron passed a relatively peaceful weekend. She had the solution finally. Safe abortion. She had made up her mind for that.

'*See the end point, not the cascade of events.*', she told herself. She had a lot to thank God for he brought Sofia in to knowing her closely. She had availed a definitive solution for her worst problem in her entire life. Born and grew-up Orthodox Christian, Meron knew very well what was right and wrong in the eyes of God. But, she had remnant concerns as a mother. She opened a dialog with herself. '*It is not that I want to kill my baby, it is that I don't want to kill myself. God, you know what had happened to me.*'

The father of her baby was a rattle snake indeed. He had poisoned her with a potent neurotoxin - rape allaying with unwanted pregnancy.

Continuing the pregnancy was not going to be only about the disruption of her union with Jovani. It was not going to be about her mental health only. Even if she delivered safely, her child would live with an early adversity-Identity crisis. Meron learned this from a TEDx Talk that she followed on Balageru TV a week ago. The show was about the impact of early adversity in life. The speaker was a famous pediatrician in the US and in the world, Dr. Nadin Burke. She is known for her incredible breakthrough in determining the effect of early adversity in humankind. The title of her talk was "How childhood trauma affects health across a lifetime".

"Early adversity, be it sexual abuse, physical trauma, child neglect, or having a parent with mental illness, is significantly associated with significant morbidity and mortality in life according to the strong evidence extracted from our study.", she drew her conclusion.

Early adversity–identity crisis was already there in Meron's circle, endangering her baby, unless she discontinued the pregnancy. She didn't want to raise a baby badly affected by that adversity. What is more, all the cruelest people she had ever known in her life, from soldiers to leaders, they had identity crisis. She clearly understood the scale of early adversity endangering the life, of her offspring. She saw safe abortion as the only anti-dote that she could have timely to reverse the fate of her pregnancy.

She had survived the acute phase of rape trauma syndrome successfully. The shock. The denial. The panic-attacks. Suicidal ideation. All had vanished from her brain. But her problem was far away from over unless and otherwise she discontinued her unintended pregnancy.

It was 100% appropriate for Meron to call her family members in Eritrea and tell them what had gone wrong with her. If she couldn't tell her mother and father, then she could have shared it to her only sibling, Dawit who was 3 years younger than her. But, she decided to keep them all unaware of everything. She was no different from the thousands of women across the globe who become victims of rape and unintended pregnancy and remain silent, year in, year out.

Telling them the bad news of her rape trauma and unwanted pregnancy was going to definitely sound like the death of a fiancé before her wedding day. One cannot mourn her death laud. Meron didn't want to mess the good news of her getting married to a successful person in two weeks' time.

Meron's decision to share the burden of her unwanted pregnancy with Sofia wasn't something that arrayed randomly. She had a horrible and unforgettable lesson. Shewit, her high-school best friend, died from complications of unsafe abortion in 2015. It happened to her, as it continues to happen today to thousands of women, who have no access to comprehensive abortion care services. She hid her unintended pregnancy from her family members and friends-including Meron. She ended up in having backstreet abortion and 3 days later she succumbed to overwhelming infection.

Meron wished that the clinic she planned to visit be like its name. She hoped it would address her concern well. St.Mary Clinic. What a beautiful name. She expected both physical and spiritual healing at it. She arrived there at 9:00 AM. The day was Monday and she was with Sofia again. The entrance gate to the clinic was wide-open. The metallic door was painted in blue-color.

The plastic seats at the reception were filled with clients. It was Sofia who prepared a card for her but they were standing together.

“Your name please?”, the card personnel asked Meron in Amharic language. The female personnel weren’t sure who the patient was and who the attendant was. Sofiya looked the client and Meron her company.

“Meron Ghirmay Haile”, Meron spoke out her full name.

“Okay age and address?”

“26, Sarbiet Sefer.”

“Okay! Take a sit please. You will be called shortly.”, the personnel told Meron to take a notice as they sat together on the waiting area.

Thirty minutes later, a bell rang. It was Meron’s turn. “Meron! Meron! Come in please!”, a soft voice called her from inside the examination room.

He was the humblest gynecologist that Sofia knew for the last three years, Doctor Desalign. Meron hurried into the room and she rapidly identified where she had to sit on.

Her heart was beating fast. She wasn’t sure whether she would tell him exactly what she wanted. He would get it in anyway. He had the talent to understand what concerned his patients’ most. He observed her once nail biting.

“Hello Meron! How are you? Welcome to our clinic!”, Desalign started establishing a rapport with his client. He was a kind of doctor who respected principles of medical practice. He never skipped steps of appropriate patient clerking.

Meron nodded her head twice. To avoid eye contact, she chose to reply to him with a body language.

"Okay! What can I help you? Feel free. I am a women's physician. I do understand everything.", he jumped to the main point that brought his client in to the clinic.

"I am four months pregnant. I came her for safe abortion. This is the ultrasound report that I had received from the Maternity Hospital I checked three days back.", she handed him her obstetric ultrasound result. She explained her problem and what she was looking for in a single statement with no space left for him to dig in to.

"I am so glad, I can help. You are in the perfect place for your need to be met.", he boosted her confidence and asked her, "Just few questions and a clarification. Why do you want to do that?"

"My pregnancy is unintended. I was rapped. My assailant had disappeared from this country shortly after he abused me.", Meron talked about her rape experience for the first time.

"I am sorry to hear about the rape. Did you try to bring him to prosecution?".

"I didn't. I had no witness. I didn't have enough information about his whereabouts neither."

"Nobody escapes from justice. In any way you need my cooperation, I will assist you for justice to be served to you. And I am happy that I can help you at least with your current problem. When was your last menstrual period?"

"My period is irregular. I think it was two months and one week back. I don't remember the exact date."

"Good. Your gestational age calculated from this ultrasound is 16 weeks and three days. What we have as an option in this case is a medication abortion.", he moved in to counselling her on the methods of safe abortion care.

Dr. Desalign continued by saying, "As far as what is available in this clinic, let me tell you this. We can only provide you a medication abortion. We will provide you an oral medication and you will take it today, right now. Twenty-four hours later, you be admitted here and you will have another tablet administered sublingually every 3 hours at least five doses and at most 8 doses in one cycle."

"What is the price doctor?", Meron shifted to cost analysis as she agreed to undergo a medication abortion.

"The cost for the procedure is 3,000-birr. It may have additional costs if the abortion process requires more than 24 hours of stay, meaning a second cycle of the sublingual medication."

"Sublingual. I don't get it doctor."

"You will hold the medication underneath your tongue until it gets absorbed into your circulation."

"Let it be doctor. You absolutely relieved my stress. God's plan. I am reborn again."

"Yes! God has a plan for everyone.", Dr. Desalign backed her remark.

"Sure, I will come."

"Good."

"Any harm that it may cause me?"

"Before you are admitted, you may experience vaginal bleeding, lower abdominal pain, or the waters could break. The abortion process might begin with this oral medication only. In such circumstances, you have to come back to our clinic or reach nearby health facility immediately. After admission, once the sublingual medication is started, you should expect to experience frequent abdominal pain for which we are going to provide you a proper anti-pain. You should also expect vaginal bleeding but your safety will be secured here as we are going to closely follow you. Vomiting and headache is also inevitable sometimes as a side effect of the medication.", Dr. Desalign finished his counselling and gave her a prescription paper.

CHAPTER SEVENTEEN

Meron had been experiencing lower abdominal pain throughout the night. She was at St. Mary clinic. She returned as she was told, after a day. It had been 24 hours since she was admitted and started taking the sublingual medication.

She didn't sleep for a minute over the night. Her face read as if she regretted. Both about her choice of the method-medication abortion and the place of the abortion care.

A terrible accident. A black lady of average height on blue pink skirt dress and a T-shirt in matching color was there, sleeping on a bed next to hers. She knew Meron very well. The lady was Martha, her friend and her former roommate. She too was there for safe abortion, admitted a day prior. A devilish coincidence. There was no way that Meron's safe abortion care could remain a secret.

"Martha! What are you doing here?", she asked her the

moment she saw her sleeping next to her bed.

“Well, what are you doing here?”, Marta questioned her back.

“Playing basketball.”, Meron teased

“The same thing. I came to the field ahead of you.”, Martha extended her friend’s tease.

“You know I and Jovani are engaged. We are not just ready for a pregnancy.”

“I know Meron. You lost contact for long. I have been following your events. You seemed too busy to turn an eye on your roommate. Here we are together going to be in pain. You ignored me. We could have celebrated the happy times together.”

“I am so sorry. I was so busy. I didn’t understand how time flied really fast. And the corona kept everybody detached.”

“Good excuse”

“No. I am serious. Anyways, back to our business. You see real friends share the hard time. Here we are together as you said.”, said Meron. They spent some time chatting about their past life together at their 4 by 4 meters room- a house rent at Lafto neighborhood.

“Good morning Meron. Would you mind if I do a pelvic examination?”, a tall brown physician who was in charge requested her. He was the slimmest physician Meron ever encountered. He was Doctor Desalign again. He was on Khaki trousers with its cuffs resting on his Monk Strap shoes.

"Oh! Doctor, please finish this problem very soon. I can't bear the pain!", Meron screamed as she held the edges of bed sheet underneath her body tighter in her both hands.

"I am sorry Meron that the anti-pain is not working properly for you. When was the time you took your last dose of anti- pain?", Desalign produced the most important question in the interest of his patient, as he prepared to perform a gentle pelvic examination.

"It was during the late afternoon at around 4:00PM.", she answered.

He became disappointed. Pain management was as equally important as the abortifacient medication itself. It is the principle of medication abortion. Nobody knew about it at the clinic, more than him. He was sure that he had ordered adequate ant-pain for his patient. The nurses must have forgotten it. The fact that Meron missed two doses of anti-pain over the night wasn't something that he could swallow easily.

"In the absence of good pain control, how can we call this a safe abortion?", he yelled at the nurse who was on duty overnight. He didn't go further to express his disappointment in front of his patient.

'Do your job now and mind about the argument later.' He calmed himself down. He went one step backwards. It was wise words that he used to follow to buffer his high temper every time he saw any mismanagement of his clients.

With the attention of her brain completely stolen by the painful uterine contractions, Meron didn't appreciate any pelvic pain as Desalign did vaginal examination on her. The findings were that there was zero percent of success of her medication abortion care. It does happen. Seeing her experience intense pain, Desalign didn't find it acceptable at least morally to let her continue another cycle of the sublingual medication. He was worried.

There was nothing that annoyed him more than a failed medication abortion. When it allayed with poor pain control, he nearly cried. In fact, his eyes were wet as he said, "I am sorry to tell you this Meron. It does happen. The medication abortion you took for the last 24 hours didn't work out. My examination revealed that the products of your conception is nowhere in the process of expulsion. Above all, I am sorry for our failure to put you on adequate pain control!"

Desalign knew that there was another better option for Meron which was surgical abortion. However, with her advanced gestational age, it was possible to have that service only at one governmental Hospital in the city of Addis. Referring her to St. Michael's University Hospital was already in his mind.

Meron's facial expression immediately changed from a frowned non-pleasant one to an expressionless disappointed one. All her hope and strength vanished when he revealed to her the progress of her abortion care. She suddenly found herself running out of energy.

"We are going to rest you for some hours and restart the whole process. Referring you to a governmental Hospital for surgical abortion is the second option. You will have your abortion care completed in a shorter period of time, compared to the time needed for successful medication abortion", he disclosed his plan of management to her opsonized with optimal counselling.

“I would better go for the referral.”, she told him her choice.

“I respect your choice. I am going to give you a referral slip. But first you need to have your pain controlled and rest for some hours before you leave. Sister, can we please provide her Diclofenac injection?”

CHAPTER EIGHTEEN

"Hello doctor! We have one suspected case of COVID-19 patient at the emergency.", a phone call consultation was made to Dr. Samuel by a final year post-graduate obstetrics and gynaecology student.

"Evidence?", he fired back at the resident.

"She has fever of 39 degree centigrade. She has severe respiratory distress; she could barely maintain her saturation with 10 liters facemask oxygen."

"Her age and does she have cough and shortness of breath?" "She is 26 years-old and she…"

"I am coming. We need to evaluate her thoroughly.", he interrupted the phone call before the resident completed his answer directed towards the question about any additional symptoms of COVID-19 in the patient.

Samuel headed to emergency room (ER), at the ground floor of St. Michael's Hospital main building and the first room found before any other service unit within the department of obstetrics and gynaecology.

He was on full stomach. Ready to combat everything. He was always like that whenever he was on duty. Saturday April 4, 2020, his duty day, wasn't busy in the morning hours. He received only two consultations that he addressed over a phone call.

At 12:30 PM the corridor of the ground floor looked like a ghost town. Dressed in green scrubs with a white gown topping it and N-95 mask covering his face, Samuel speeded towards the ER. At unbelievable pace, he covered the span of one hundred meters distance of the corridor in less than 1 minute.

A minute matters in obstetrics. Samuel emanated from that basic understanding. Through his four years stay at obstetrics and gynaecology residency, he learned to be as sensitive to respond to emergency consultations as a mother would to her baby's first cry.

"Where is she?", he asked as he entered the busy room with six emergency beds that was fully occupied with patients. He looked towards the left side of him and his eyes met the senior resident's eyes.

"Oh! She is in the triage room! She is on oxygen!", the senior resident gave his reply with a terrified look. He marched out of the room leading Samuel towards where at the critical patient was labeled a high risk suspected COVID-19 patient and isolated.

The senior resident pointed his finger to direct his senior

to her exact location from a distance of around 3 meters. Nobody dared to get close to her and evaluate her thoroughly. Samuel was sad about the senior resident's incomplete consultation. Panic attack of the virus had surfaced in many Hospitals across the city, including St. Michael's University Hospital.

"For heaven's sake, do you have full history of the patient?", he asked the senior resident in wonder

"She has high-grade fever.", the senior resident regurgitated what he said few minutes back on a phone call.

"Does she have a history of cough? Is she pregnant?", Samuel hammered the senior resident down with two more questions that he couldn't give any answer.

High-risk COVID-19 suspected case was a causal assessment in the absence of good history taking and adequate physical examination. For better for worse, first evaluation matters. The distant and superficial junior resident's evaluation misled everybody but Samuel.

Senior is always senior. Samuel thought that the patient would benefit from his close evaluation. She did indeed.

"Sorry doctor! We didn't get full history of the patient.

She was evaluated yesterday evening by a junior physician – a second year resident.", the senior resident promptly availed a cover up.

"What do you mean?", Samuel challenged him further. He wasn't going to leave him easily.

"She was kept overnight for 12 hours with a diagnosis of suspected COVID-19. She came here yesterday at 6:00

PM with a history of fever of 3 days duration. Her vital sign was stable. She was also evaluated by the COVID-19 care designated team. Their plan was to transfer her to the isolation center, and a sample for corona test is already taken."

"What was done in 12 hours' time?"

"Nothing. Test and isolation. Waiting for the result. And a plan to transfer her to the isolation center."

"What about her attendant? Any person who accompanied her?"

"She came by herself. She was relatively okay according to the previous duty team report. She looked perfectly fine except for the fever."

"A detailed history would have been helpful. Where can we get it from now? Any cough or shortness of breath?"

"No respiratory complaint. Her oxygen saturation was good. She started to deteriorate two hours back."

The patient stopped breathing right before their eyes amid their discussion to settle her diagnosis. "She is in cardiac arrest! Please help! CPR!", Samuel bellowed as he rushed to do advanced life support for her. He only wore N-95. He had no face shield. Yet, he volunteered to resuscitate the patient without adequate personal protective equipment (PPE).

"She is COVID-X, a Do Not Resuscitate case. The recommendation is do not resuscitate any high-risk suspected case of COVID-19 patient. Available scientific evidence shows that only as low as 14% of COVID-19 patients did receive CPR when they had in hospital-cardiac arrest. Eighty-eight percent of those who received CPR didn't survive", a new voice came from within the room. He was Doctor Henok, emergency medicine final year post-graduate student. He was consulted as soon as the patient arrived. He returned on the next day to check her progress.

He saw the patient before Samuel but from a distance. He was briefed about the patient by the duty residents a day before. And it was the same information as that was presented to Doctor Samuel. It was Henok's suggestion to isolate the patient as a highly suspected COVID-19 case once he heard from those duty residents.

"This young patient needs an urgent care. Whatever!", Samuel disputed while his hands continued in motion, doing the rapid and deeper chest compressions.

"Why would I jump to COVID-19", he made his stance about the patient's diagnosis clear.

Aron, the short but thick senior resident was in green Scrubs as his senior and he was too not on adequate PPE, as he reluctantly joined Samuel in doing CPR. Three minutes later, one nurse volunteered to assist them.

CHAPTER NINETEEN

"Continue bagging! Bagging! Non-shockable rhythm has just emerged on the monitor!", Samuel yelped.

He was thrusting the palm of his right hand on the patient's chest and his left palm was resting on the dorsal surface of his right hand. He compressed stronger and stronger and faster. The light of hope of reviving the patient was at the end of tunnel.

"Alright!", Aron responded. He squeezed the self-inflating adult Ambu Bag connected to 100% oxygen in his right hand while he stabilized the face mask. He could see the patient's chest rising intermittently, which confirmed right flow of oxygen into her lungs.

A beeper from the Pulse Oximeter started to make noise abruptly. The peripheral pulses of the patient returned. Her pulse rate was read as 140 beats per minute.

“Intravenous fluid. One bag of normal saline on the right IV line and another bag through the left IV line. Hurry-up!”, shouted Samuel as the patient made her first gasp after 15 minutes of CPR. Aggressive fluid resuscitation continued. Two liters of intravenous fluids was instilled into her circulation.

The beeping of the monitor grew into a disturbing noise but it was for good. Oxygen saturation of the patient exceeded 90% with face mask oxygen. She had irregular spontaneous breathing. The wall-watch at the emergency room rang. It was 1:00 PM.

Aron counted both her respiratory rate and pulse rate at the same time. Sixteen breaths per minute and 120 beats per minute, respectively. Through the two large bore IV cannulas secured in the brachial veins of the patient, additional two liters of normal saline was pumped in. She was only in her 25th minute of post-cardiac arrest. Wonderful teamwork. Lucky patient. Skilled and knowledgeable physicians. Medicine is skill plus knowledge plus luck. Absolutely correct, according to Samuel’s experience in medical practice. The luck could be the patient’s or the physician’s.

The patient started to respond to pain. She had regular breathing. Her blood pressure displayed on the monitor was 80/50 mm Hg.

‘Yes!’, Samuel exhaled. The blood pressure was not recordable few moments back. Superb. It was an effective resuscitation indeed. Precisely, as his initial consideration.

“Our patient is revived! Finally. Thanks to God and thanks everybody in here.”, he asserted. In one hour, the patient articulated incomprehensible words for the first time and her blood pressure became normal, 90/60 mm Hg. By this time, she had four liters of intravenous fluid administered in to her circulation.

"Resuscitate and correct circulation. It does work colleagues. Successful CPR. Isn't it beautiful day?", he conferred with his colleagues who participated in the resuscitation.

"Yes! It is beautiful. I wouldn't eat lunch and dinner today. I am totally gratified. Let's not forget to provide her potent intravenous antibiotics.", he further conveyed his satisfaction while he gave a new order. Aron stood on his side with delight.

Everybody's heart became filled with the joy of saving the patient. Samuel knew there was a hard work to be done to find the cause. The patient was awake and ready to give her word. First, her consciousness had to be assessed.

Samuel's green Scrubs had turned blue black soaked in splash of sweat. He took a deep breath.

"What is your name?", he asked the patient.

"Meron Ghirmay.", she answered.

"Where are you?"

"At St. Michael's Hospital."

"What time is it?"

"Lunch time."

Meron answered all questions correctly. She confirmed the regain of her consciousness the best way possible. He proceeded with doing complete physical examination.

Before doing that, he asked all the staff in the triage room to leave except Aron. He closed the door. Patient's privacy was a principle in his blood all the time.

He checked her eyes and her conjunctiva was pink. That easily ruled out anemia from the picture. He checked her chest and her lungs were clear. No sign of chest infection. He moved to her abdomen and he gently palpated it and, "Oh It hurts doctor.", Meron responded.

"I am sorry."

"Not at this moment. I had a miscarriage a week back."

"Where? At home or at health facility?"

"It was at home. After the passage of the conceptus tissue, I had continuous vaginal bleeding that stopped after few days."

"Why didn't seek medical advice? When did you start to have fever?"

"I had it for the last three days."

"Would you mind if I do vaginal examination for you. I am going to do it gently. It is going to be helpful. We need to know the cause of your fever."

"Is it not corona infection Doctor?" "It doesn't seem so."

"I thought it was corona. I came here yesterday in the afternoon."

"You are right. Fever this time is being considered Corona unless proven otherwise. I fear you have a problem much more dangerous than corona."

"What? What do you mean doctor? More dangerous than corona virus."

"Yes, a chronic serial killer and more fatal to young women like you than COVID-19. I am looking for that. Can I do vaginal examination first?"

"You can doctor."

Samuel wasn't astonished at the findings of his vaginal examination. There was a foul-smelling vaginal discharge. It was something that he suspected though not fully. He finally found the cause for her shooting fever. It is a known killer, which takes the lives of thousands of women every year. Septic abortion was the final diagnosis that he was able to settle with all his arguments and hard work.

Miscarriage followed by vaginal bleeding and then fever. He used his finding of foul-smelling vaginal discharge to confirm his diagnosis. Before he went out to reveal his findings to his colleagues outside the triage room, he had to share every bit of information about it with his patient. His patient had the right to know everything about her problem. And he was well versed to practice that basic human right.

"Meron! We fully understand your problem now. You have severe sepsis inflicted by unsafe abortion. You are likely to have some products of concepts retained in your womb. We need to do Ultrasound.", he disclosed to her what he was up to with his examination.

"Does that mean I am corona free?", Meron questioned him.

"We will see the result of your COVID test. Corona is indirectly killing young women. With an excuse of corona, women are dying from complications of pregnancy. You are lucky and strong Meron. But why didn't you go to a health facility early before the infection became severe?"

"I went to a private clinic to have a safe abortion. Almost ten days back. They gave me an oral medication first and I was admitted 24 hours later for inpatient abortion care. I was provided sublingual medication for 24 hours which failed. I went back home and a day later I started to have vaginal bleeding accompanied by frequent abdominal cramps. Soon I had witnessed passage of the conceptus tissue. As I stated after few days, the bleeding stopped and I thought it was over."

"And then?"

"Then I developed fever. Oh! I forgot. I was referred to this Hospital initially from a private clinic for completion of my abortion care through a surgical method once the medication failed."

"Why didn't you come then?"

"My friend advised me not to come to this Hospital."

"My goodness! Why did she give you such advice?"

Meron tried to recall how and why she didn't respect Doctor Desalign's early referral to the Hospital. After one minute of silence, she had the whole sequence of events figured out in her mind as it was, as it took place.

It all began with Sofia's phone call on March 29.

"Good morning Meron!"

"Good morning to you too!"

“I just called to tell you something very important.”

“And what is that?”

“They masked it but the truth had come out finally. St. Michael ‘s is dangerous now. It has become corona virus infection rampant Hospital.”

“My doctor has told me that I shouldn’t take time and it is very important. Are you telling me to abandon my referral to the Hospital?”

“Yes. Meron you better die from natural causes than COVID-19. We can handle your problem any other time.”, Sofia alarmed her with her two-line statement.

“A physician from the Hospital was talking about it in an interview on TV yesterday. He demonstrated that no service is compromised at the Hospital due to corona and he gave his advice that clients shouldn’t have any hesitation to seek medical advice at the Hospital.”, Meron forwarded her justifiable argument with fresh evidence.

“You don’t know these people. They were lying. I am telling you. A nurse, a friend of mine who works at the Hospital has informed me that 50 health personnel from the Hospital, including 20 doctors are already infected with the virus. The nurse himself is COVID-19 positive now.”

“I don’t believe you?”

“You should. What you watched on TV and what we hear in the media is just a joke. Inviting patients to receive care at a center where the infection is contracting health personals themselves. The authorities must have lost their minds.”

“Oh My God! What is going on?”, Meron wondered.

"When one doesn't take care, it is inevitable. You don't take a shower to sleep on a mud. Right?", Sofia contained her friend's wonder in a net of well-articulated reasoning.

"You are correct Sofia.", Meron started to trust her friend.

"Can you imagine? 20 doctors are infected with Corona virus now.", Sofia brought up a living proof about how dangerously COVID-19 was widely spread at the Hospital. And that completely convinced Meron not to make any attempt to show up at the presumed COVID-19 rampant Hospital again.

"*I don't want to die*", a strange but meaningful song played in her head, suddenly. With all the trauma and pain, Meron wanted to survive. Her seek for safe abortion care was interrupted in the middle. And fake news about the spread of the infection was the cause.

Misled by the health professional's fake information but with evidence, she finally accepted her friend's advice. To avoid a risk of death in around less than 2 % of the time, she stumbled into a well-studied danger of carrying unwanted and unplanned pregnancy.

Even though Meron was able to rehearse the whole phone conversation, she decided to brief Samuel only on the key statement that made her change her mind, as a result of which she refrained from visiting St. Michael's Hospital on time.

"My friend received an information that the infection was spreading in this Hospital. The source was a trustworthy person, a nurse who works here. She told me that he warned her that this Hospital was too risky to be visited by clients.", she delivered the truth to him.

He was not surprised. It was something that he fully anticipated to hear about. He had addressed the issue well once, during a panel discussion.

CHAPTER TWENTY

A cold morning in March of 2020. Unlike the wishes of many residents of the city, the cold weather in Addis didn't improve even in the month of March. More than in any other month in the calendar year, it was desired to get hotter with the perspective of the Corona virus outbreak. Hot weather was perceived to be unsuitable for the virus at the beginning of the pandemic.

The virus had to be an evil work according to that common perception. Because, it arrived with a perceived weather of its preference. How could that be by chance? It was unanswered question to those residents.

At 10:30 AM in the morning, the city was as quite as it had never been before. A report of a surge in cases of corona virus in the city compelled some restrictions to be imposed. What was feared could happen started to surface. Sunday's

March 28, 2020 show on Saba television was broadcasted, as planned.

"Good morning our followers everywhere! In our today's show, March 28, we are going to have a panel discussion on maternal care, family planning, and comprehensive abortion care services in the time of COVID crisis. On behave of our followers, I would like to thank Doctor. Samuel from St. Michael's University Hospital, Doctor Lidya Seare from Addis Ababa University Black Lion Hospital, and Doctor Osman Abdella from St. Paul's Hospital Millennium Medical College", a panel discussion was opened by a female host on Saba Television.

Samuel was already three months into his family planning fellowship training at St. Michael's University Hospital. Beautiful three months filled with a privilege. He celebrated his success at the interview through the whole month of January. The results of the interview were announced a week later, as it was initially planned.

Family planning fellowship medical education and a clinical service, he adored the combination very much. He never saw any blessing beyond that.

Samuel's childhood dream was to become a medical doctor. It happened and it was at his dream medical school.

Among other things, Samuel loved rap music. Tupac's "Brenda's Got a Baby", the second single from his debut album 2Pacalypse Now, was his favorite rap song.

Say something repeatedly, you will become it sooner or later. The contents of the lyrics of the song become absorbed into his blood stream through time. He used to sing the song as early as the time he joined medical school.

"Brenda's Got a Baby"

I hear Brenda's got a baby

But, Brenda's barely got a brain

A damn shame, the girl can hardly spell her name

(That's not our problem, that's up to Brenda's family)

Well let me show ya how it affects the whole community

Now Brenda really never knew her moms and her dad was a

Junky, went in death to his arms, it's sad 'cause I bet

Brenda doesn't even know

Just 'cause your in the ghetto doesn't mean you can't grow (you can't grow)

But oh, that's a thought, my own revelation

Do whatever it takes to resist the temptation

Brenda got herself a boyfriend

Her boyfriend was her cousin, now let's watch the joy end

She tried to hide her pregnancy, from her family

Who didn't really care to see, or give a damn if she

Went out and had a church of kids

As long as when the check came they got first dibs

Now Brenda's belly is gettin' bigger

But no one seems to notice any change in her figure

She's 12 years old and she's having a baby

In love with the molester, who's sexing her crazy

And yet she thinks that he'll be with her forever

And dreams of a world with the two of them are together,

Whatever, he left her and she had the baby solo

She had it on the bathroom floor and didn't know so

She didn't know, what to throw away and what to keep

She wrapped the baby up and threw him in the trash heep

I guess she thought she'd get away, wouldn't hear the cries

She didn't realize

How much the the little baby had her eyes

Now the baby's in the trash heep balling

Momma can't help her, but it hurts to hear her calling

Brenda wants to run away

Momma say, you makin' me lose pay

The social workers here everyday

Now Brenda's gotta make her own way

Can't go to her family, they won't let her stay

No money no babysitter, she couldn't keep a job

She tried to sell crack, but end up getting robbed

So now what's next, there ain't nothing left to sell

So she sees sex as a way of leaving hell

It's paying the rent, so she really can't complain

Prostitute, found slain, and Brenda's her name, she's got a baby

Samuel found the message in the sound track applicable in his society, though it had been more than 25 years since it came into existence. Maybe not in the same way as Brenda, but many young girls from his city, from different walks of life, were becoming victims of unintended pregnancy.

That was a serous gap that he fully palpated and made him unhappy, as he attended his obstetrics and gynaecology specialty training at St. Michael's University Hospital. The rap song was a great inspiration for him, part of his motivation to apply for the family planning fellowship program, although he didn't mention it both in his motivation letter and interview.

The success of filling that gap, through the abilities he expected the fellowship program would arm him with, would represent 75 % of his satisfaction of living his life as a physician, until the end of time.

Born and raised in Addis Ababa, he adored everything in the city. The city of love and hospitality is well-known for the quality of social life in it, where the rich and the poor communities of the city live in love and peace. Its modern infrastructure comprises of numerous towers, sky scriptures, five-star hotels, modern bars and clubs, and wide high ways.

Samuel loved the city for the good people who resided in it, more than for the beauty of its modern infra-structure. However; like in any other mega-city in Africa, there was one thing that everybody hated about the city, including him. It was the traffic jam, the number one reason that lead him to reside close to his area of work. He resided in Haya-Hulet neighborhood and he enjoyed a 15 minutes' drive to and from the Hospital from his home.

Money making being ill-suited to his mentality and determination, he threw up all the advantages of working at private Hospitals in Addis Ababa city. He made a conscious decision of serving at St. Michael's university Hospital, where he completed both his undergraduate and post-graduate medical training. It was for a fair payment but that didn't go beyond covering his house rent, day-to-day expenses, and fuel for his 2010 Yaris- Belta car.

"Doctor Samuel first, what is the impact of this COVID crisis on the maternal care including family planning and comprehensive abortion care services? Can you tell us the African perspective of the pandemic.", Sara, the female TV host forwarded her questions to the first panelist. French twist was a perfect hair style that she picked to be hers for the day.

"Let me start by thanking you for your invitation and the opportunity you gave me to speak. To address your question, the impact of the crisis is significant enough to cut the number of clients attending maternity care units by half across the continent of Africa.", Samuel instigated his discussion.

He continued further by saying, "I regret that we are coming forward late. How useful it would have been had we had this panel discussion at the start of the pandemic. In our Addis Ababa city, we have seen some late arrivals of mothers with hypertensive disorders due to the pandemic When it comes to family planning, a record of 30% decline in uptake has been observed. The other issue, is a disinformation about safe abortion services and as a result there is a significant decrease in the number of clients looking for that service."

"I am sorry to interrupt you Doctor Samuel, what is

this disinformation all about? What do you think is the ultimate solution?", Sara urged him to detail her about the disinformation.

"There is wrong information about the shutdown of safe abortion services due to the pandemic. It is absolutely ridiculous. What killed thousands of women in the past will definitely bounce back and kill even more. Yes, we have to be careful about the corona outbreak but we know what kills our women most. In the name of COVID-19, there is no reason to stop the lifesaving services."

Samuel was indirectly talking about the dangers of the commonest causes of maternal mortality. Unsafe abortion, the fifth cause of maternal mortality worldwide, had never been a joke. And in the time of COVID-19 pandemic, it was only going to get worse. Many women like Meron, were falling victims to complications of unsafe abortion in the shadow of the corona crisis. That was Samuel's concern since day one, about the pandemic.

"Thank you, Doctor Samuel, for your in-depth explanation. Just one question before I move to the second panelist. What is your message to the women out there about the maternity and family planning care in this difficult time of crisis?", Sara asked him to finally deliver his take-home message.

"Ahem! Ahem!", Samuel coughed two times impulsively and his N-95 was seen getting fully inflated. Everybody in the TV studio panicked. He was on brown suits and white shirt with brown ties with white strips. He chose his brown loafer shoes to be a match to his suits and tie. For few moments, nobody seemed to care about how stylish he looked. "Hhhhhh...Don't be shocked. I don't have corona. I just cleared my throat", he jested.

Shortly, he went on to state his take home message explicitly by articulating, "I would like to inform mothers to continue their regular antenatal care follow-up visits. Please attend your deliveries in a health facility. Nothing is compromised in the maternal health service provision. The same is true for family planning and safe abortion care. We know that you might have fear but we do follow standard COVID-19 infection prevention measures while we make sure we continue to provide these essential health services."

The other panelists took control of the podium turn by turn but they didn't seem to add any more message, apart from additional scientific evidence that supported Samuel's message.

CHAPTER TWENTY-ONE

Sofia stood by the door side that lead to the gynecology ward. The halve-glass half-aluminum door was halve-closed. But, for those attendants who wanted to violate the rule of not going through the door in the absence of a legitimate paper, the door was half-open.

Sofia choose to negotiate with the strict person who controlled the entry door to the ward, who only knew only two signals, like a computer. One and zero. He was like '*You have permission paper, go on!*' '*You lack permission paper, hold on!*' There was no way of making him have a purple heart.

Before she leaned to negotiate with him, she spotted one physician coming towards the direction where she was located. She stared at him with her non-blinking eyes.

They were completely strangers to each other. She was about to say a name that was very familiar to both of them. Before she said it, he said it laud.

"Are you Meron's family member? Are you the one who accompanied her?"

"No. I just arrived now.", she replied with her slurred speech.

"She is okay now. It is a long story. I suppose she told you that she was in a near to death situation yesterday. Please follow me and you can see her condition with your own eyes.", Doctor Samuel guided her to the room.

Meron was transferred to the gynaecology ward two hours earlier. She left the emergency room at 6:00 AM. She underwent a surgical procedure, manual vacuum aspiration (MVA), through which remnant conceptus tissue was removed from her uterus, as soon as she was transferred to the gynaecology ward.

In her twenty-fourth hours post-cardiac arrest, Meron showed remarkable improvement. She was conscious. Her vital signs were normalizing except fever. She was still on parenteral antibiotics.

"Thanks God! Thanks God!", screamed Sofia the moment she found her friend sitting in her bed.

In few seconds, they were in a tender hug. They looked like a sick child and a caring mother. It was an emotional reaction. They could do nothing but disrespect the rules of coronavirus infection prevention in the Hospital. Their eyes were washed in tears.

Sofia already knew that her friend had spontaneous miscarriage at home following the failed medication abortion at the private clinic. Seven days after the miscarriage, both of them had no clue that complications of the miscarriage could arrive late.

Any delay beyond her presentation to the Hospital could have proved to be fatal. So would have any further delay after her arrival in the Hospital.

CHAPTER TWENTY-TWO

Samuel made himself ready to make a ward round. He complied with the strict infection prevention protocol developed to abide every health worker in the Hospital. He put on his face mask and respected social distancing. He respectfully requested Sofia to leave the room for a moment. Time was up, 9:00 AM.

Meron had been in the gynaecologic ward for 7 days, recovering. She had completed her intravenous antibiotics treatment. She looked glad and gratified. If there was another best thing that Sofia had ever done for her, it was bringing her the newspaper. What she read minutes back on Bisrat Newspaper gravitated her towards full healing. Both in flesh and in soul. A phenomenon Addis Ababa police report issued on April 10, 2020 under ‘Police and People’ column was something that very much belonged to Meron.

"Today we captured the anaconda of human trafficking in this country. Nick-named as Rambo, his real name is John Tewlde. A criminal doesn't do his job in halves. He is also a serial sex offender. His neighbors at Bole neighborhood were completely stunned. They knew him as a good person. He is sentenced to serve life in prison.", briefed Capitain Bekel- Deputy Inspector General of Addis Ababa police.

"Any woman who was abused by the person whose picture is displayed can make a toll-free call at 84849 and submit her accusation. He is already prosecuted but it would be helpful to inspect his inner and outer circle. He has many associates who helped him to commit all the crimes. They will too be in custody soon. Already one is arrested.", he added.

Meron read the police report in detail, with great passion and high concentration. She had every reason to be very pleased. The morning of her 7th post-cardiac arrest day showed up with a good news of arrest of her assailant. Not only that but she also came to know his identity and his notorious criminal network.

Meron was among more than a dozen women who were sexually abused by John. She wanted to jump in happiness as she saw his picture pinned in the newspaper along with the report. But she didn't do so on purpose. Nobody knew what that police report meant to her and her friend Sofia was with her on her side, as she went through the report. She didn't want anybody to track down the whole story of her misery in Shire town.

John was captured in the capital Addis, following three months manhunt imposed by the city's police. He was found guilty of human trafficking and sexual abuse. Locked in chain, he was already serving his life in prison sentence.

For seven years, he lived his life in luxury at Bole neighborhood. He enjoyed raping victims at different places of his network, including at refugee camps. He had a shameful extraordinary addiction for assaulting women wherever and whenever he felt he was safe to do it and escape without being convicted.

Addis Ababa police made a breakthrough in cracking his unbreakable criminal network by arresting one of his associates who was assisting him in accessing beautiful women secretly in Shire town. Dejen, Meron's high-school friend, the person who conspired to make her victim of sexual violence, was John's strong affiliate.

Dejen was detained at Bole international airport while he tried to leave Ethiopia with a forged passport. He was interrogated by the police until he spat out the name of his boss and the unspeakable crimes they committed together as a team.

Bringing sex offenders to justice does help victims of sexual abuse well. It had just started to work for Meron. All her emotional dust was settled. John was already done. She would love to give information about Dejen, her high school friend, the Judah who deceived her. "*Everything has time.*", she spoke to herself.

John's rape addiction drove him to jail. Soon, it could take him to his grave before he lived to serve life in prison. It was possible. What killed a billionaire abuser at random, could kill a multimillionaire sex-offender electively. He had to only take a look at what happened to Jeffery Epstein.

John worked in the business of human trafficking for 10 years. He had many agents whose job stretched beyond Sudan to Libya and Europe. With a short cut of abusing human beings, he climbed to sense the life of a multimillionaire.

"Good morning Meron! It is beautiful that you are doing well. Your COVID test is also negative.", said Samuel. He got ready to fully counsel her.

"Good morning doctor! That is great.", she reacted.

"You see you, you returned from the doorstep of death. Many women like you don't make it to live again.", he immediately began on what he held on his agenda for her before she was discharged from the ward.

"Correct. I have a lot to thank my God and You. God bless you doctor.", she complied.

"Can you imagine that 22,000 women die from complications of unsafe abortion globally every year?"

"So sad."

"These deaths are totally preventable."

"Would you mind elaborating it more to me?"

"If women can access effective contraception and comprehensive abortion care services, we can stop this high mortality year in, year out."

"I was raped."

"I am so sorry to hear this. I am here to help you with all

my best. Would you mind telling me the whole story."

"It all happened in mid-November, about four months ago."

"Was the perpetrator arrested? Nobody escapes from justice. It is only a matter of time.", Samuel pointed out.

"No. He disappeared from this country after the incident."

"Why didn't you report to police immediately? Did you check in a health facility soon after?"

"He first put me under the influence of alcohol. I was not conscious. So, I did not."

"Did you check any health facility after you gained consciousness? You could have used emergency contraception; it can be used up to five days after unprotected sexual intercourse."

"He used condom. So, I thought I would be safe."

"Condom is a reliable sexually transmitted infections prevention method but it is one of the less effective contraceptives."

"Doctor! Would you please give more clarification?"

"Condom has a high failure rate at preventing pregnancy, as high as 17%. You see Meron, it is a basic human right for a woman to have control over her body. She can do that by putting herself on reliable effective contraceptive methods such as implants and intrauterine device (IUD). Even after a rape incident, it is not too late to be on effective contraception. Emergency contraception like emergency contraceptive pills or plan B and copper IUD provides a last chance to prevent pregnancy after unprotected intercourse. Pregnancy test and safe abortion is an option if this last chance is missed."

CHAPTER TWENTY-THREE

Meron's eyes bulged and her knees buckled in shock and disbelief. She wanted to scream but it wasn't the right time. She suddenly pulled out of the consultation with Doctor Samuel. Impossible. She saw Jovani hurrying through the corridor. He was in the Gynaecology ward. He was searching for her bed number and her room.

"I want you to do me a favor. My husband is here. He is completely unaware about this all. He was supposed to be in Italy. I don't know how he happened to be here.", Meron appealed to her doctor.

"My pleasure and my Job."

"He is for sure here to discover something. He cannot check my wellbeing by making a surprise visit."

"If he asks you anything, please don't tell him about my

abortion, near death situation, and my rape experience."

"Patient-doctor confidentiality. No way. I am going to keep it a secret. It is your right. Patient's right."

She felt her heart beat faster. Her breathing became rapid. She felt her throat getting drier. The door swung. Her handsome Jovani emerged from the doorstep. He wasn't handsome this time. He looked furious and his beard was not cut. His hair too. He looked like a Muslim clergy. After being disconnected from her for three weeks, there he was physically. Meron couldn't just believe what her eyes were seeing.

"Amore Mio! Surprise! Scusa! What happened to you! I feel heart-broken.", he opened his mouth before he took the first step toward her from the doorway. She started to cry. He run to hug her. He pulled out a napkin from his pocket and dried her eyes. They huddled together for two good minutes.

"I suffered from a pelvic infection. I was so sick. I didn't call you because, I didn't want to bother you. You also called me several times but I didn't answer it for the same reason.", replied Meron with a nasal voice. Her nostrils were already congested.

"What! This is not acceptable. I am your fiancé, and soon would be your husband. I should have helped you as you passed through this difficult time."

"I know honey but I didn't want to worry you much."

"Why didn't you go to a private health facility?"

"I thought they wouldn't treat me well as a presumed Corona patient with my fever. I also talked to Sofia."

“Did she accompany you?”

“No. It is hard to help people closely in this time of corona crisis. But, she gave me wise words that I should visit this Hospital.”

“I am understanding you!”

“How did you know I was here?”, she asked him.

“I am glad to find you like this. I thought you were very sick. Thanks to God, I found you in a good condition.”, he replied.

“How about our Dad Lazeroo?”

“Thanks to God. He miraculously recovered. He slept in ICU for 20 days. God is good.”

“How did you know that I was sick and I was here”, she reverted to her previous question.

“I made a call to Sofia. I tried to call you multiple times but your phone wasn’t working. She told me that you are at St. Michael’s Hospital.”, he lied. “What else did she tell you?”

“That you suffered from corona infection.”, he lied again.

Jovani came to the hospital to confirm whether what somebody told him about her was true or not. The person leaked the head and tail of Meron’s secret abortion care and post-abortion care.

Samuel studied the reaction of Jovani. He easily understood how to carry out what his patient appealed for.

“Hi! Jovani! I am Doctor Samuel!”, he chimed in their

conversation.

"Nice to meet you doctor. Thank you for saving my fiancé."

"I did my job. I am ready to leave. Is there anything you need to hear from me?"

"Can I talk to you in private? Scusa amore!", Jovani inquired.

Some people lie. Only doctors lie to save life. Samuel kept his promise with accuracy. In the corridor of the ward, he recited what Meron apprised Jovani of, moments back. He mentioned to him that Meron's problem wasn't related to complications of pregnancy.

Jovani suspended his suspicion. He regretted. He confessed to his God and hurried back into the ward.

"Honey! We are going to have our weeding as scheduled. Your doctor said that you are going to be discharged today.", he cheered her up.

"May God let it be!", she exhaled.

She wanted to dance in joy inside the ward. She had survived triple tragedy. Rape. Unintended pregnancy. Cardiac arrest. Jovani had no clue about all that.

"Meron! I can't wait to marry you.", said Jovani.

"Get me out of this Hospital on a white bride dress if it is possible.", she joked.

Index

europe books